SOVA

A Machines of War Novel

First Edition, Published in 2025

ISBN eBook 978-1-0670627-0-5

ISBN paperback 978-1-0670627-1-2

Please contact the author directly for distribution/wholesale queries:

Stephen.beath73@gmail.com 0064 0274 715 002

Dedication

To my wife, Sabrina, whose motto of JFDI (Just F'ing Do It), coupled with unwavering support and love gave me the motivation to make this book happen.

To my daughter, Charlotte, whose laughter and energy brighten every corner of life.

And to my son, William, who faces the challenges of Beckwith-Wiedemann syndrome with strength and courage that words cannot capture.

Introduction

The year is 2036. The world has been devastated by war, as superpowers wage an unrelenting conflict with AI-driven war machines dominating the battlefield.

Ukraine, once vibrant, is now a shattered wasteland of obliterated cities and broken promises. Peace treaties have long since crumbled, and the fight for survival has become desperate.

Russia, once led by Vladimir Putin, has morphed into the Rusviet Empire, controlled by a ruthless faction known as The High Commissariat. Their vision is clear—total domination and the enslavement of Europe. Ordinary Rusviets, powerless under the regime, yearn for peace, but defiance is met with brutal force. Prisoners of war and civilians alike are shipped east, forced to work on the production lines that build the war machines of their oppressors.

Now, in Western Ukraine, the last free city—Lviv—stands on the brink. Rusviet forces are closing in. If Lviv falls, so does the last hope of resistance.

But amidst the chaos, one machine remains—an advanced war machine, long thought lost, waiting for the right pilot to rise...

Table of Contents

Chapter 1 – Awakening

Dimitri shivered as the sun dipped behind the dark, forested slopes of the nearby blue mountains. As he inhaled, he could almost taste damp leaves and pine needles mingled with wood smoke from the orphanage nestled at the base of the hill.

This hilltop had always been his retreat, and the ancient tree standing there, with its thick, twisted branches, felt like a guardian, offering him a sense of safety. Leaning into its gnarled trunk, he closed his eyes, letting the familiar rough bark press into his back.

Even the tree couldn't silence the distant booms of war that echoed through the valley. Each thunderous roar sounded closer than yesterday, reverberating throughout the forest like an ominous drumbeat. He opened his eyes, squinting into the fading light, searching the horizon for any sign of movement, any hint of the Rusviets' long-anticipated arrival. Another shiver, though it wasn't just the evening chill. As the sun dipped lower, casting long, skeletal shadows from the forest, he felt the creeping advance of the war that had been coming ever since he could remember.

The earth trembled beneath him. Startled, Dimitri jumped to his feet, his uneven legs protesting the sudden movement. An earthquake? No ... He shook it off, though his heart continued to race. The bell from the orphanage rang out, signalling dinner. He sighed, casting one last glance at the sky before he began the slow, familiar trek down the hill.

Dimitri's limp was pronounced – one leg longer than the other, a reminder of a disability that had haunted him since birth. His gait was awkward, and each step down the uneven slope sent a jolt of pain through his hips. He bit his lip and kept moving, weaving his way through the trees towards the excited noise of children rushing to eat.

As he neared the orphanage, the familiar clamour of the dinner rush surrounded him. Kids jostled and yelled, sprinting towards the large double doors, their movements quick and fluid. Dimitri's steps were slower, more deliberate, his limp painfully evident in moments like these. The other kids' eyes darted to his legs.

A voice, cutting through the noise, called his name – soft but clear, like it came from the wind itself.

'Dimitri …'

He froze, knitting his brow, and turned to look back up the hill. There was no one there, just the rustling leaves and the dark silhouette of the ancient tree against the setting sun. The voice echoed in his ears, impossible and strange.

Before he could make sense of it, something struck him hard from the side. The impact sent him crashing to the ground, the breath knocked out of him. Pain seared up his spine. He lay there gasping, the mocking laughter of the other kids mingling with the fading echo of his name, the mysterious voice having vanished.

Vladimir stood over him, his small, weaselly eyes gleaming. The boy's round, colourless face twisted in amusement as he watched Dimitri struggle to get up.

'What's the matter, Dimock?' Vladimir sneered, emphasizing the derogatory nickname with mock concern. 'Lose your balance again?'

Vladimir, stocky and intimidating, leaned in closer, his voice whispering darkly. 'Must be hard walking on legs like those.' He gave a theatrical limp as he sauntered around Dimitri, exaggerating his movements. The other kids laughed along with him, their faces lit with the thrill of witnessing the humiliation.

Dimitri's cheeks burned with shame, but he forced himself up, biting back any retort. His body hurt from the fall, the side of his face grazed, but he wouldn't give Vladimir the satisfaction of seeing him stay down.

'Go on, cripple,' Vladimir hissed, lips curling into a cruel smile as he limped away dramatically. 'Maybe one day, you'll learn how to walk properly.' His laughter rang out as he swaggered off towards the orphanage doors, leaving Dimitri alone in shame.

He stood, the world spinning around him as the other kids ran into the orphanage, a tall grey and imposing building that was decaying and cold. Then, through the fading laughter and the noise of running feet, he heard a distinct sound. A low rumbling – the sound of trucks approaching.

'Dimitri.'

He turned to look up the hill at the gnarled old tree at the top, but no one was there.

Before he could investigate further, Dimitri heard the trucks getting closer, their headlights piercing the falling darkness as they snaked along the road towards the orphanage. He spotted the emblem of the two-headed eagle on the trucks' front grill, unmistakably belonging to the Rusviet Empire. A twist of panic gripped him, rooting him to the ground.

Then came the unmistakable, metallic clatter of a machine moving with swift precision – a chilling sound like claws scraping against the earth. Emerging from the forest was one of the Rusviet's infamous S10s, nicknamed the 'Velociraptor' for its slim, angular frame, the height of an adult human, but eerily reminiscent of the deadly dinosaur. He could see the machine guns mounted on each arm as it trotted alongside the military trucks, halting near the orphanage entrance. Its sensors swept the area, pausing as it locked its glowing red gaze on Dimitri.

Cold fear gripped Dimitri's throat. He turned in defiance and, with trembling legs, climbed the hill towards his safe space at the top, disappearing among the trees. Within seconds, he heard hard boots hit the ground.

Without looking back for fear of being spotted, he could hear them – soldiers. Voices barking orders. The front door to the orphanage being kicked open. Finally, the cook Ulma's voice, rising above the din. She was shouting at the soldiers, her voice full of anger and fear.

'No! You can't take them! These are children!'

Dimitri's heart raced. He wanted to run down the hill, to stop them, but his legs wouldn't move. All he could do was watch from a distance as the soldiers forced the children into trucks. The Velociraptor stood sentry, guns following each child as it passed. Ulma was still shouting, resisting as they dragged her with them. Tears streamed down Dimitri's face as he crouched low, approaching the old tree at the top and rounding it, hiding from sight. He felt utterly helpless.

It was nearly dark now. The ground beneath him began to tremble, Dimitri's breath catching in his throat. He heard a strange clicking sound, which grew louder, mechanical and rhythmic. He stumbled back, eyes wide, heart racing faster than ever before. The torch beams from the soldiers swayed at the bottom of the hill, the men's shouts still faint in the distance. But Dimitri's focus was entirely on the ground at his feet. Something moved beneath the earth.

Abruptly, the hilltop split open with a crack. He yelped, scrambling backwards as dirt and small rocks tumbled down around him. From the centre of the hill, a few meters from the tree, a large, metallic, dark blue shape began to emerge.

As the head of this machine rose out of the soil, a pair of glowing yellow lights flickered on, scanning the area. Dimitri felt his legs lock in place. He couldn't move. His mind screamed at him to run, to flee down the hill, but his body refused to obey. The lights turned towards him, and for a moment, he thought he heard a voice, faint and mechanical, whispering through the cold night air.

'Dimitri ...'

He gasped. How did it know his name? He blinked, convinced he was imagining things, but the voice came again, louder this time.

'Dimitri … come closer.'

It wasn't a command, not really. There was something strange about it. Something … familiar. The massive metallic frame shifted, and a cockpit hatch slowly began to open with a hiss, revealing a dark interior. The blue glow from inside the machine pulsed softly, almost inviting.

Dimitri hesitated, glancing down the hill towards the soldiers. There were now only a couple near the truck. The rest had their torch beams sweeping up the hill, nearing him. They would find him soon. Worse still, the Velociraptor was nowhere to be seen. His heart hammered against his chest, torn between the unknown danger of the machine and the very real threat of the soldiers.

The smooth surface of the machine's body shone in the reflected moonlight, dirt falling off its side as its voice whispered again.

'Dimitri, I can save you from soldiers, but you'll need to trust me and get in before it's too late. I'm an AWMa, also called Advanced War Machine, Series a, on the side of the Resistance. I can help you escape.'

With one last glance at the soldiers below, who by now had clearly spotted them, Dimitri made his decision. He stepped forward, hands trembling as he placed one foot, then the other, into the hollowed-out cockpit. The metal felt cold beneath his touch, but as he settled inside, the space seemed to mould around him, adjusting for his small frame. The controls hummed to life, the seat wrapping around his body like a protective shell. The cockpit sealed shut with a quiet thud, locking him inside.

The AWMa's voice came again, but this time, it spoke directly to him, reverberating through the walls around him.

'Welcome, Dimitri, you're now safe.'

Several Rusviet soldiers crested the top of the hill, rifles in hand, torches flaring brightly at the cockpit.

'Get out, get out,' the lead Rusviet commanded, his deadly machine gun pointed right at the cockpit. Dimitri didn't move, too terrified to speak or act.

'Dimitri, I can help you escape, but you'll need to give me your permission,' spoke the machine, slowly, quietly. The soldier who issued the command, sensing what was about to happen, raised the butt of his gun and slammed it into the cockpit. It glanced off without leaving a mark. Dimitri recoiled, somehow managed a squeak. 'AWMa, get me out of here.'

The machine jolted slightly, as if shaking off years of sleep. Dimitri gripped the armrests, feeling the powerful vibrations beneath his feet as the giant machine fully emerged from the earth, towering over the group of soldiers who stepped back in awe. He glanced around, the view from inside giving him a new perspective. He could see the whole hill, the orphanage, and the dark shapes of the soldiers running back down the hill.

'What are you?' Dimitri whispered, barely able to speak through the fear tightening his chest.

The AWMa's response was calm, almost soothing. 'I'm your guardian. I'm going to get you to safety.'

Dimitri felt a surge of something unfamiliar – a strange mixture of fear and hope. For the first time since the war had reached this part of the country, he felt the slightest bit of control over his fate.

The giant shifted, and Dimitri could feel the power beneath him, the raw energy coursing through the machine. It was waiting for his command. Before he could think about what to do next, the AWMa spoke again.

'They are going to come for us again.'

Dimitri glanced down the hill, his breath catching as he saw one of the soldiers shouldering what looked like a missile, pointed right at them.

'What do we do?' Dimitri whispered.

The AWMa's lights brightened. 'We run.'
The soldier fired. A trail of smoke streaked through the dim evening air as the missile roared towards them.

'Brace yourself,' the AWMa's voice said, steady, almost calm, though Dimitri's heart pounded in his chest.

The giant spun on its heels, its massive form moving faster than Dimitri thought possible. With an instinctive precision, it twisted its hulking frame, positioning its back to the incoming missile. Dimitri could only watch, helpless, as the world outside blurred. Then, the impact.

The missile slammed into the giant's shoulder, exploding in a brilliant flash. The cockpit rattled violently, sending Dimitri flying against the restraints. His vision blurred, and a high-pitched ringing filled his ears. The blast sent a wave of heat and debris across the hill, bits of metal and dirt cascading down as smoke billowed into the darkening sky.

Dimitri blinked through the chaos, eyes wide, trying to catch his breath. The AWMa had taken the hit directly, shielding the cockpit – shielding *him* – from the full force of the explosion. Outside, the machine's metal plating was scorched and dented, but it remained standing.

'Damage minimal,' the AWMa reported coolly. 'We need to move now.'

Before the soldiers could recover, the giant took off, its massive legs carrying them down the opposite side of the hill. Dimitri clutched the armrests, his whole body shaking as the machine thundered forward, each step jolting him inside the cockpit. The world around them turned into a blur of shadows and flickering lights as they sped down the slope.

'We're headed for the forest,' the machine explained. 'It will provide cover.'

The trees loomed ahead, their twisted branches stretching out like skeletal fingers. As they neared the edge of the forest, Dimitri could hear the soldiers shouting, their voices growing fainter behind them. Torch beams sliced through the smoky air, but the soldiers wouldn't reach the treeline in time.

Just as Dimitri thought they might escape, the unmistakable metallic clatter returned – the Velociraptor. It moved through the underbrush with frightening speed, weaving between trees like a predator stalking its prey. Its glowing red eyes scanned the darkness, locking onto Dimitri and Sova.

The AWMa crashed deeper into the woods, branches snapping and breaking under its weight. Dimitri flinched as the machine ducked and wove through the thick trunks, its movements surprisingly agile for something so large. Twigs and leaves scraped against the outer shell. Dimitri felt like he was being carried through a nightmare.

Behind them, the Velociraptor followed relentlessly, its smaller frame darting between trees. The twin machine guns mounted on its arms whirred to life, sending bursts of gunfire towards them. Sparks flew as bullets ricocheted off the giant's armour.

'Hold on,' the AWMa commanded. 'We'll soon be out of range of the soldiers.'

But the Velociraptor wasn't giving up. It launched its own shoulder-mounted missile, the telltale whine cutting through the forest like a banshee's scream. Dimitri's heart pounded in his chest as the giant machine veered sharply, dodging the missile just before it slammed into a nearby tree, sending a fireball and splintered wood flying.

Behind them, the forest seemed to close in as the missile's explosion faded. The Velociraptor was still on their trail, but the soldiers' shouts were swallowed by the dense underbrush.

The AWMa halted abruptly, its sensors flaring in warning. Dimitri crouched low inside the cockpit, his heartbeat pounding in his chest and the darkness of the forest wrapping around them like a thick blanket. The sounds of the pursuit had faded, but the forest remained eerily still, too still.

'I think we've lost it,' Dimitri whispered, peering out through the trees.

The AWMa's voice came low and steady. 'No. It's close.'

A sudden rustle ahead sent a chill down the boy's spine. From the shadows, the Velociraptor emerged, stepping into view as if it had been waiting for them all along. Its red gaze locked onto them, the machine's slim, predatory frame eerily still save for the quiet whirring of its servos. It had predicted their route, lying in wait like a skilled predator.

For a second, neither moved. Then, the forest erupted. The AWMa fired first, unleashing a volley of rounds from its chest-mounted cannon, lighting up the dark with streaks of muzzle flash. The Velociraptor reacted instantly, disappearing behind a massive tree, its small frame agile as it took cover.

Without hesitation, the AWMa lunged forward. Dimitri held on tightly as the war machine crashed through the underbrush, closing the distance in a few heavy strides. Instead of firing again, the giant moved with a calculated fury. It reached the tree where the Velociraptor was hiding, its enormous frame slamming into the trunk with a force that shook the ground. Dimitri felt himself thrown forward in the cockpit, before the restraints snapped him back into his seat violently.

The AWMa didn't stop. Its powerful arms wrapped around the tree trunk, catching the Velociraptor in a deadly embrace on the other side.

The smaller machine struggled, its twin machine guns whirring to life, firing aimlessly, but it was too late. The AWMa tightened its grip, metal screeching against metal as it crushed the Velociraptor in its grasp. A horrific, eerie mechanical scream echoed from the smaller machine, its frame buckling and contorting under the pressure. The sound was like a dying beast, unnatural and haunting.

With a final, bone-rattling crunch, the AWMa's arms tightened one last time, and the Velociraptor fell silent. Its crushed remains slumped in the giant machine's grip, sparking weakly as it was reduced to twisted, broken metal.

Dimitri exhaled, his pulse still racing. 'Is it … dead?'

'Disabled,' the AWMa confirmed, its voice quiet and measured. 'We must continue to a safer place, deeper in these woods.'

Chapter 2 – Sova

The AWMa, towering but graceful in its movements, continued deeper into the forest for some time, until finally, they reached a small clearing by a stream, the moonlight casting long shadows across the forest floor.

'This will do,' the machine's voice spoke gently, in contrast to the mechanical precision it normally carried. The giant machine crouched low to let Dimitri out.

The cockpit hissed softly as its canopy began to lift, and he felt the cool night air rush in. Slowly, he unbuckled himself from the seat and climbed out, feeling the soft earth.

The forest was quiet, but it was the kind of quiet that made Dimitri feel small. The trees loomed above him like silent giants, their branches whispering in the night breeze. The cool air carried the damp, earthy scent of moss and pine, mixed with the faintest hint of wildflowers, as though the forest itself was breathing around him. He stood for a moment, taking it all in. He was free of the machine's cocoon, but the world around him felt as dangerous as the one he'd just left behind.

'Is it safe?' Dimitri asked, looking back at the AWMa.

'For now,' the machine replied. 'But we must remain vigilant. The Rusviets are likely still searching for us.'

Dimitri took a few steps away from the machine, his mind swirling with everything that had happened: the orphanage, soldiers, Velociraptor, and this strange machine. He wasn't sure what to make of any of it.

'Why … why are you helping me?' Dimitri asked, turning to face the AWMa's massive frame.

The machine hesitated, its mechanical eyes glowing faintly in the dark. 'You activated me. My previous pilot did not return, and I was unable to continue my mission.'

Dimitri frowned. 'What happened to him? Your pilot?'

The AWMa lowered its head slightly, its gaze turning downward. 'He left the cockpit to forage for supplies. The Rusviets captured him.'

Dimitri felt a lump form in his throat. He didn't know what to say. 'How long ago was that?'

'Several years ago,' the machine responded. 'After my pilot's disappearance, I went into hiding. My communication systems were so damaged I could not contact my command. So I buried myself beneath the hill, where I remained, waiting for a new pilot or orders that never came.'

Dimitri's heart sank. The AWMa had been alone for all that time, a ghost, forgotten by both sides.

'I'm sorry,' Dimitri whispered. He wasn't sure why he said it, but he meant it.

The AWMa's glowing eyes lifted to meet his gaze. 'There is no need for apology. It is the nature of war.'

Dimitri hugged his knees to his chest, staring out into the dark forest. 'You have a name?'

'I was designated AWMa-077, Advanced War Machine, series a. But my pilot called me something else. A nickname.'

Dimitri turned his head, curious. 'What was it?'

The giant hesitated, as if recalling a distant memory. 'He called me "Sova." It means "owl" in Rusviet. My systems are optimized for nocturnal operations.'

'Sova,' Dimitri repeated softly, testing the name on his tongue. He liked it. It felt right. 'Can I call you that?'

'If you wish,' the AWMa – Sova – replied.

Dimitri managed a small smile, though it quickly faded as thoughts of everything he had lost washed over him. The orphanage, all his belongings, Ulma. Everyone was gone. His home was gone.

Sova's sensors hummed quietly before she responded. 'Your family ...' she began, her tone slightly shifting, as though she were searching through memories. 'Do you remember them well?'

Dimitri hesitated. 'My parents?' He swallowed, eyes distant. 'I was only seven when they were taken. I can barely remember what they looked like now ... but I remember how my mother used to hold me. She'd sing to me when I couldn't sleep.' He paused, voice growing quieter. 'And my father ... He used to lift me onto his shoulders, and I felt like I could see the whole world.'

Sova remained silent, listening as Dimitri spoke, her sensors trained on the boy's trembling hands.

'They were brave,' Dimitri continued. 'I remember them telling me not to be scared, even when the soldiers came. But … I was scared. And now, they're gone.' He squeezed his eyes shut, fighting back tears.

There was a long silence, and then Sova spoke. 'The world can take much from us, Dimitri. But it cannot take what we remember. You carry that with you, in every step. In every choice.'

Dimitri nodded, absorbing the words, feeling an unexpected warmth despite the ache in his chest. 'What do you think we should do?' he asked, looking up at the towering machine.

Sova was silent for a moment, then spoke with quiet certainty. 'Behind the seat,' the AWMa's voice directed him gently. 'There's a bag. Retrieve it. It belonged to my pilot.'

Dimitri hesitated before climbing back into the cockpit and pulling out a rugged canvas bag from behind the pilot's seat. The bag felt heavier than he expected, the contents clinking softly as he set it down on the ground. Inside, he found an assortment of survival tools, a sleeping bag, and a compact pistol that felt cold and heavy in his hand.

As he examined the contents, something caught his eye: a patch sewn into the inside flap of the bag, faded but still legible. 'Lt. Viktor Novik,' it read, the name of the pilot before him.

'Viktor was always prepared regardless of environment.' Sova's voice carried a hint of sadness. 'But you are here now. And you will need these things to survive. Begin by gathering firewood. There are berries to the west of this clearing – safe to eat. I'll keep watch while you prepare.'

Dimitri nodded, feeling comfort in the machine's presence. He gathered some branches and twigs from the forest floor, his fingers numb from the cold as he worked. The quiet of the night wrapped around him like a blanket, only broken by the crackle of Viktor's firestick as Dimitri struck it against a stone, igniting the kindling into a small, warming flame.

He built a makeshift shelter using the waterproof sheet and a few sturdy branches, setting up his sleeping bag inside. The forest was dense enough to provide some protection from the wind, but the shelter would offer a little more. Sova meanwhile stood sentinel-like at the edge of the clearing, her mechanical limbs locked into place but sensors still scanning for danger.

As the fire crackled, Dimitri broke the silence. 'Sova, am I your pilot now?'.

'Yes,' Sova replied softly. 'But enough talk for tonight, rest. Tomorrow we move again. Together.'

Dimitri nodded, lying back in the sleeping bag, feeling the warmth of the fire against his face. The fatigue of the day's battles pulled him towards sleep. Before his eyes closed, he looked once more at the AWMa, her silhouette outlined against the moonlit forest. In that moment, Dimitri realized something had shifted.

For the first time since he had climbed into Sova's cockpit, he no longer felt alone.

Chapter 3 – River

Dimitri's stomach growled loudly, breaking the heavy silence of the still morning.

'How long have we been here?' Dimitri asked, pressing a hand against his stomach. 'Approximately eight hours,' Sova replied in her even tone. 'Your blood sugar levels are low. You need more food.'

Dimitri groaned. 'I need more than just food. I need a decent bed!'
'Time to go westward. It'll be safer once we reunite with the Resistance,' Sova said reassuringly.
Sova moved with a speed that Dimitri could hardly believe. Massive as she was, her giant body moved catlike through the trees, barely disturbing the branches. Dimitri clung tightly to the seat, heart thundering in his

chest. Despite seeing no sign of soldiers, Dimitri knew they weren't out of danger yet.

Inside the cockpit, a series of glowing screens lit up, displaying maps, sensors, and a live feed of the surroundings outside in all directions. Dimitri's head spun trying to make sense of it all.

'What-what is all this?' Dimitri stammered, voice barely audible above the hum of the machine.

'These are your operational systems. I will guide you through them when needed. For now, we must focus on our escape.'

Dimitri nodded, still shaking from the events of the previous night.

He swallowed hard, his fear rising. 'I'm … I'm not sure I understand. You want me to go on a mission with you?'

'Drones detected,' Sova said. 'Three Sui 77 Red Vipers – enemy aerial combat units.'

Dimitri's stomach twisted. He'd heard about Red Vipers from the other kids at the orphanage and seen on news channels the destruction they left behind. These Rusviet drones were lethal, fast, and relentless.

He looked through the glowing cockpit window, breath catching as he saw the shadowy forms of the drones approaching, their triangular shapes silhouetted against the dark sky.

'Are they after us?' Dimitri asked.

Sova responded with mechanical precision. 'Yes. Red Vipers inbound from the north. Estimated time to contact: fifty seconds.'

Dimitri's heart pounded. 'What do we do?'

'First,' Sova said, 'we must hide.'

The machine shifted, and Dimitri could feel the powerful motors beneath him adjusting course. They moved faster, the landscape blurring past. Trees whipped by, their branches slashing at the cockpit window. Dimitri squinted, trying to keep up with what was happening as Sova suddenly angled downward, crashing through the thick underbrush.

Ahead of them, the ground gave way to an expansive river, its waters deep, dark and cold under the morning sky. Dimitri instinctively held his breath as Sova splashed her massive frame into the water, sinking beneath the surface as she couched low on the deep riverbed in the middle of the river. The cockpit remained dry, but the cold pressure of the river pressing against the hull was unmistakable. Water sloshed against the window and over it as they sank beneath the surface. The early morning sunlight glittered above them through the moving surface of the river.

'They won't be able to detect us in the water,' Sova said, her voice calm, though Dimitri couldn't help but feel a growing sense of unease.

He nodded, the cold fear in his chest easing slightly. For the moment, they were safe. He pressed his head back against the seat, trying to catch his breath.

The relief was short-lived.

A sharp beeping noise filled the cockpit. Dimitri sat up, eyes wide as the screens flashed red again.

'Heat signature detected,' Sova reported. 'Our power core is giving us away.'

Dimitri's stomach flipped. 'Can't we turn it off?'

Sova's response was swift. 'Negative. Disabling the power core would leave us defenceless.'

Dimitri swallowed hard, watching as the outlines of the Red Vipers drew closer on the map. The drones would be on top of them any second now.

'What do we do?' Dimitri asked, gripping the armrests.

'We fight,' Sova replied. Her voice was steady but laced with something unfamiliar – an edge of tension. Even this machine could sense the danger.

'Prepare for missile launch,' Sova continued, her cockpit lights shifting from soft blue to glaring red. Dimitri's glanced at the controls, fingers trembling, unsure of what to do.

'Tracking systems engaged. Locking onto enemy drones.'

Dimitri watched in stunned silence as the screens lit up with targeting information. Each Sui 77 was marked with a glowing red icon, rapidly closing in. Sova's tracking systems moved with precision, placing crosshairs on all three drones at once.

'AGM-92 Surface to Air Missiles locked,' Sova reported. 'Firing in three ... two ... one ...'

Dimitri's entire body jolted as the AWMa launched a barrage of three 'Dragonspear' missiles from her shoulder-mounted pods. The cockpit vibrated, the missiles streaking upward, out of the water, and cutting through the air. Dimitri's eyes followed their path on the screens.

There was a sudden, blinding flash of light. One drone exploded in midair, followed by a second. Dimitri watched the debris rain down into the nearby forest.

The third drone still approached.

Dimitri's breath stopped, panic set in, as the last drone dove towards them, its sleek form lit by the sun. Its wings cut through the air, the whir of its engines loud and menacing as it lined up for an attack run.

'Missiles reloaded,' Sova reported. In an instant, the shoulder-mounted missile launchers deployed and fired – two streaks of light tearing through the sky. The Red Viper banked hard, dodging the first missile. The second barely missed its tail as it dived towards the river.

'Impact imminent. We're out of missiles,' Sova warned. Dimitri barely had time to react before the Sui dropped what was unmistakeably a bomb, its sleek, metallic casing glinting and a set of stabilising fins protruding from its sides.

The explosion was deafening. The blast wave slammed into them with the force of a tidal wave, Dimitri's world turning to chaos. The shock hit him like a physical blow, the air knocked from his lungs as the cockpit violently shook. Metal screamed as Sova's entire frame jolted backwards, the force of the blast sending her tumbling onto her side.

Dimitri struggled to orient himself, trying to breathe through the rising panic. The cockpit lights flickered and his vision blurred, the water outside swirling like a violent vortex.

The drone circled back and dove towards them, tracer fire coming from its red wingtips, the sharp crack of bullets slicing through the water's surface. Each round slammed into Sova's armour, rattling her frame. Dimitri's eyes darted to the cracked cockpit screen. The small fracture from the blast had deepened, spidering across the glass. Every hit made the crack tremble, tiny splinters of glass flaking off and threatening to shatter completely. The drone passed overhead, preparing to return for the final assault.

Sova pulled herself upright, standing in the river with her upper frame above the water to allow the cannon to engage.
'Tracking systems offline.' Sova's voice sounded tense. 'Manual control required.'

Dimitri's eyes widened. 'What? What do I do?'

'Take control of the cannon,' Sova instructed. A new set of controls lit up before him, displaying the cannon's manual targeting system. Dimitri's hands hovered over them, unsure.

'Focus, Dimitri. You can do this.'

Dimitri swallowed hard and gripped the controls. He had never done anything like this before, but he knew he had to try. As he pulled the controls upward, he detected movement of the cannon barrel rising from the chest of the machine.

He locked onto the approaching drone as it moved at high speed towards them, its sleek body illuminated on the screen. His eyes narrowed as he adjusted the aim of the cannon, aligning the targeting reticle with the drone's path.

'Fire now!' Sova commanded.

Dimitri's squeezed the trigger, feeling the jolt of the cannon as it roared to life. The shot went wide of the incoming drone. Panic surged through him as Sova jerked under another impact, the Sui's rounds slamming into its armoured frame. Warning lights flashed across the cockpit, and Dimitri could see cracks widening in the cockpit's reinforced glass.

'Come on, come on,' Dimitri screamed. He could feel Sova's systems struggling, armour plating groaning as it absorbed hit after hit. The heads-up display flickered, the red warning signals blurring together as the damage reached critical levels. Another direct hit rocked the cockpit, and Dimitri felt a rush of air through the cracks. He blinked away tears, unable to tell if they were from fear or the sting of the cold wind.

Out of nowhere, a sharp whistle pierced the chaos. Dimitri barely had time to react before a missile streaked from the shadowed treeline, its tail a trail of smoke. It struck the Red Viper dead on, erupting into a fireball that lit up the sky. The explosion sent shards of metal and debris scattering, crashing into the river, and the impact wave pushed Sova back a step, almost toppling her.

Silence followed, broken only by the crackling of flames and the faint sound of water lapping at the bank. Dimitri stared in disbelief. He blinked. Slowly, the pieces fell into place. They weren't alone.

As the drone's wreckage smouldered in the river, Sova began to emerge from the water. Her hydraulics hissed, joints creaking as she climbed up the muddy bank. Water poured from her armoured plating in steady streams, each step sending ripples throughout the ground.

'Damage report,' Sova intoned, her voice calm despite the chaos. 'Primary systems operational. AGM-92

Surface to Air Missiles depleted. M-60 Autocannon ammunition at 12%. Left leg actuators showing signs of strain from the blast – mobility slightly impaired, but manageable.'

Dimitri wiped sweat from his brow. 'Who fired that missile?'

'Friendly fire, but as to who, it's anyone's guess,' Sova replied. 'We must retreat for now. I've detected a structure nearby – a barn, likely abandoned. It will provide temporary shelter.'

Sova moved swiftly, her silhouette cutting through the thick forest as she navigated the dense underbrush. Branches snapped underfoot, but her movements remained eerily silent for something her size. Dimitri, still strapped in the cockpit, felt every bump as they weaved through the trees, Sova's eyes scanning the landscape.

Soon, through the treeline, the outline of an old, weathered barn came into view. Its roof sagged, and patches of moss clung to the rotting wood.

As they approached the barn, Dimitri unclipped his harness and slumped back in his seat, eyes staring up at the cockpit's ceiling. The echoes of the battle still rang in his ears, and the memory of his helplessness during the last encounter gnawed at him.

He couldn't just sit there, relying entirely on Sova. If he was going to survive, he needed to do more.

'Sova,' he said quietly, his voice filled with uncertainty, 'back there … I didn't know what to do with the weapons. I just froze. How do I get up to speed? How do I – how do I get better?'

Sova's eyes glowed softly on the console, her voice calm but firm. 'Acknowledged. You are learning, Dimitri, but more practice is needed to fully integrate with my systems. I can initiate a simulated combat scenario. Would you like to begin?'

'Sova, I want to replay it,' Dimitri said, knowing most Ai's can capture, record and even replay events they witness, his voice carrying a trace of desperation. 'The river scene. The attack drone.'

Sova's eyes blinked softly, as if considering his request. 'Very well. Initiating simulation. Recreating Sui 77 engagement at the river. Prepare yourself, Dimitri.'

The cockpit flickered, and Dimitri was suddenly back in the river. The waters shimmered below the cockpit, reflecting the approaching Sui 77 as it thundered across the sky, just as it had in real life. He could almost feel the same rush of panic that gripped him then.

'Take control of the M-60 20mm Autocannon,' Sova instructed, her voice cutting through his spiralling thoughts. 'This time, anticipate its movement. Aim ahead of the target.'

Dimitri's hands tightened around the controls, sweat forming on his brow. He lined up the shot, his heart pounding as the Red Viper drew closer. This was it – his chance to prove he could do it, to prove he wasn't just a scared kid in a war machine.

He squeezed the trigger, and the cannon roared to life, tracers lighting up the sky as they arced towards the Sui. In that split second, the Sui 77 shifted, banking sharply to the right. Dimitri's rounds sailed past harmlessly, vanishing into the sky.

'Missed,' Sova reported, her voice devoid of judgment. 'You hesitated, Dimitri. Again.'

Frustration welled up inside him. 'I had it,' he muttered, anger directed more at himself than anyone else. 'I thought I had it.'

'Adjust your angle,' Sova continued, unwavering. 'And focus. You have to lead your target, not follow it.'

Dimitri tried to steady his breathing, tried to push down the doubt that was creeping back in. 'Run it again,' he demanded, voice hoarse. He wasn't ready to let go, not yet.

The Sui 77 looped back, resetting its approach as if mocking his failure. Dimitri lined up his shot once more, his finger hovering over the trigger. This time, he waited, watching, trying to predict the machine's next move. He fired again.

The rounds came close, closer than before, but still missed, streaking past the Sui as it veered off, untouched. Dimitri slammed his hand against the console, tears of frustration blurring his vision.

'Why can't I do it?' he choked out, his voice barely audible. 'Why am I always missing?'

'Because you're afraid,' Sova replied, her tone gentle. 'Afraid of failing again. But this is how you learn, Dimitri.'

Dimitri wiped his eyes angrily. He hated this feeling, hated how powerless he felt, but deep down, he knew Sova was right.

'Enough,' Dimitri murmured, voice raw. 'Show me … show me the orphanage simulation.'

'Are you certain?' Sova asked.

'Yes,' he replied, the word laden with emotion.

The scene changed, and Dimitri was suddenly looking
down from the hill, at the orphanage, the very place
where his world had fallen apart.
He saw the soldiers and Velociraptor, and there – standing
in the centre – was Vladimir. The sight of him was like a
punch to Dimitri's gut.

He raised his hand to the fire control stick, moving the
sights onto Vladimir, his fingers trembling as they
hovered over the trigger. It would be so easy, just one
shot … just one.

But he couldn't do it. The weight of all his failures, his
anger, his sorrow – all of it pressed down on him, and his
hand fell away from the controls. His shoulders shook,
and he turned his face away as tears slipped down his
cheeks.

'I'm sorry,' he whispered, more to himself than to Sova.
'I'm so sorry.'

Sova's voice softened, almost maternal. 'Emotions are
not a weakness, Dimitri. They remind us of what we fight
for.'

Dimitri sat there, silent, letting the tears fall. This was his struggle, his burden. He knew too, somehow, that this was just the beginning of learning how to carry it.

'Take some time to forage for food,' Sova said. 'There should be edible plants nearby, maybe some small game. Use the pistol. You can check the surrounding area for berries and firewood.'

Dimitri grabbed the pilot's bag, slinging it over his shoulder, but paused as he noticed something different in Sova's tone. 'What about you?' he asked. 'You never seem to stop. Don't you need to recharge or something?'

Sova's optics flickered briefly, and she replied, 'I do require periods of deep sleep. While I am designed for endurance, maintaining my systems and processing vast amounts of data requires regular cycles of hibernation. If I do not rest, my performance will degrade. My power core, while nuclear, still needs to regulate itself, and this downtime allows for internal repairs and recalibrations.'

Dimitri blinked, surprised by the admission. 'You sleep?'

'In a way,' Sova explained. 'My core functions slow, and non-essential systems shut down. It's not unlike your sleep, but I remain semi-aware, able to detect threats if needed. This 'deep sleep' is essential for maintaining my combat readiness and long-term functionality.'

Dimitri nodded, digesting the information. 'How long do you need to rest?'

'I'll manage with short intervals for now, but extended combat will necessitate longer periods. While you forage, I will enter a brief cycle. The good news is I've identified how to fix the targeting system. No offense, Dimitri.'

Dimitris cheeks burned with shame. 'That's okay, Sova. Better you take the next shot than me'.
'You'll master the fire control system, Dimitri. I have absolutely no doubt.' Sova replied gently.

She moved slightly, crouching low, adjusting as her servos powered down, and the cockpit hatch opened with a soft hiss, letting Dimitri out.

'Understood,' Dimitri said, hopping onto the ground. 'I'll be back soon. Don't … oversleep or anything.'

A small, humanlike chuckle emanated from Sova. 'I'll be awake when you return. Gather what you can. We will need it for the journey ahead.'

As Dimitri stepped out into the forest, the knowledge of Sova's need for rest settled over him like a new layer of understanding. This war machine, so powerful and seemingly unstoppable, had its own vulnerabilities – just like him.

Chapter 4 – Operative

The afternoon sun filtered through the dense canopy as Dimitri made his way back towards the barn, a bundle of wild berries and firewood in hand. His boots crunched softly on the forest floor, the air warm but heavy with the lingering tension of the morning's battle. Every step brought him closer to where Sova lay hidden at the tree line, her hulking frame nestled in the shadows.

He paused when he reached her. Sova remained crouched low, her once-glistening armour dulled by mud and debris from the riverbank skirmish. Her systems had powered down into deep sleep, a necessary reset to repair internal damage from the drone attacks. The usual hum of activity inside her had faded, replaced by an eerie silence. Her optics, normally alive with light, were dim, the AI war machine slumbering like a living being.

Dimitri watched the motionless form of his unlikely companion. He could feel the weight of the morning's battle still pressing down on him – his limbs ached from the strain, and the memory of the cannon's recoil buzzed in his hands. Sova had saved them again, but now, for a few hours, it was his turn to stand guard.

He headed towards the barn, pushing the door open with his shoulder. The warm, dry air inside was a relief after the chaotic dampness of the river, but the barn offered little else in the way of comfort. Dimitri set down the berries and firewood, his mind racing with thoughts of what had happened and what might come next.

He barely had time to settle onto the hay-strewn floor when he felt something cold press against the side of his neck. His body froze as his mind registered the sensation – a knife.

Dimitri's slowly turned his head, squinting against the sunlight filtering through the barn's wooden slats.

The man lowered his knife and gave a quiet laugh. 'Relax, kid. If I wanted to hurt you, I wouldn't have taken out that Red Viper by the river.' He slid the knife into a sheath on his thigh, his sharp eyes scanning Dimitri's face. 'You're the one piloting that metal giant taking its Deep Sleep, aren't you?'

Dimitri sat up, rubbing his eyes. The man before him was older, possibly in his late forties or early fifties. His face had the deep lines of a man who had clearly lived a tough life, his sharp features softened only by the small grin playing on his lips. He wore a patchwork of tactical gear, and his eyes gleamed with a mix of amusement and curiosity. He exuded a grandfatherly affection, despite his hardened edges. A faint accent marked his Ukrainian origins.

'Who are you?' Dimitri asked, voice shaky.

The man sat back on his heels, offloaded a large pack and what appeared to be a sleek missile launcher from his back, and offered a hand. 'Name's Maksym. Ukrainian Special Forces, or what's left of it. You're Dimitri, right? Been watching you and your mechanical friend from a distance.' He pulled a packet of dried meat from his jacket, tossing it towards Dimitri. 'Eat. You look like you haven't had a proper meal in days.'

Dimitri hesitated but took the food, his stomach growling despite the tension. He gnawed at the meat, watching Maksym with wary eyes.

'You've got guts, kid,' Maksym said, standing up and stretching. 'Piloting that thing on your own? Not many people could do that.'

'How do you know about Sova?' Dimitri asked, swallowing hard.

Maksym chuckled. 'I've seen enough action to know a war machine when I see one, even from miles away. Sova is impressive, but she's not invincible. Hiding like that means you're trying to avoid the Rusviet patrols. Smart move.'

Dimitri nodded, still unsure of the man's intentions. 'Why are you here?'

'Same reason as you, I expect,' Maksym said, pacing the floor of the dilapidated farmhouse. 'To fight back. The Rusviets have an armoury nearby, supplying weapons for their final attack on Lviv. That city's the last bastion of freedom for us, and if it falls, Ukraine's done for. I've been scouting the area, trying to find a way to take it down.'

Before Dimitri could respond, a low rumble emanated from the woods, deep and ominous. The ground trembled beneath his feet as something massive stirred in the shadows. Sova was powering back up, her systems responding to the spike in Dimitri's heart rate. Through the window, Dimitri could see Sova emerging from between the trees like a ghost in the dappled sunlight. Her footsteps echoed with a heavy, deliberate rhythm that sent ripples through the air.

Dimitri scrambled to his feet, heart pounding. Sova advanced, her towering silhouette casting a long shadow over the clearing. The machine's eyes, twin orbs of glowing yellow, locked onto Maksym, analysing him in a cold, calculating manner.

'Maksym, move!' Dimitri shouted, but his voice came out hoarse, barely a whisper in the tension-filled air.

Maksym froze, his only movement a slight shift of his stance towards the war machine. His eyes narrowed, but he didn't back down. He readied his body to spring into action, but even he knew there was no escaping a machine like this.

Sova's frame stood just thirty meters away, the sunlight glinting off its armour like the sheen of a predatory animal stalking its prey. A cold intelligence glimmered behind those eyes, and Dimitri felt a wave of dread: Sova was calculating, sizing up Maksym as a potential threat.

Without warning, Sova's right forearm rotated, revealing a hidden compartment. With a sharp mechanical whir, a long, menacing barrel extended outward, unfolding into a sleek, multi-barrelled minigun. It clicked into place while the low whir of the gun's rotation filled the air, the weapon spinning to life.

'Sova, wait!' Dimitri shouted, panic surging through him. He waved shaking hands in front of the machine, trying to regain control. But Sova's eyes remained fixed on Maksym, her targeting systems assessing every movement, calculating the threat level with unnerving accuracy.

Neither Maksym nor Dimitri dared to breathe. The forest around them had gone still, even the wind holding its breath. Dimitri heard only the soft whirring of the minigun barrels, like the growl of a beast ready to pounce.

Maksym's gaze flickered from Sova's glowing eyes to the minigun pointed at him, his jaw tightening. He was a trained special forces operative – he knew the kind of firepower that Sova could unleash. There was no escaping it. But instead of running, Maksym stood his ground, raising his hands slowly, palms outward, in a gesture of surrender. His eyes met Dimitri's, a silent understanding passing between them.

'Dimitri.' Maksym's voice was calm, too calm for the situation. 'You need to call it off.'

'I'm trying, Maksym!' Dimitri stammered, his voice cracking with fear.

'Calm down, Sova. He's not a threat. Maksym's was the one who fired the missile at the Sui by the river,' Dimitri pleaded, sweat dripping down his face.

Sova hesitated, the whirring of the minigun slowing, but the barrels continued to spin. The machine's internal systems were conflicted, trying to reconcile Dimitri's emotional distress with the data it had gathered on Maksym's combat capabilities. Every second felt like an eternity.

With a soft mechanical click, the minigun slowly retracted back into its compartment, folding away with a hiss of hydraulics. The tension in the air broke, and Sova's stance relaxed, the glow in her eyes dimming.

'Sova …' Dimitri muttered, forehead glistening. 'What was that?'

'Apologies,' Sova's voice rumbled. 'Your elevated stress levels triggered an automatic defensive response.'

Maksym, doing his best to appear unphased by the looming war machine, stepped back with a grin. 'Ah, the legendary Sova herself. I've heard stories about you'

Sova's voice hummed through the cockpit speakers, steady and calm. 'Thank you, Maksym, for helping us eliminate the drone threat.'

Maksym raised an eyebrow, a wry smile tugging at the corner of his lips. 'She talks, too. Impressive. Although, judging by the damage to your cockpit, it looks like you could use some repairs.'

Sova's frame shifted, her massive weight pressing into the soft earth beside the farmhouse. ''Tis but a scratch,' Sova replied, her tone more light-hearted.

Maksym chuckled but quickly turned serious. 'Actually, I do need your help – both of you. Given I saved your skin on the river, I hope you'll hear me out.'

'Go on,' Sova spoke gently.

Maksym took a deep breath before continuing. 'I've been tasked with finding and neutralising a Rusviet armoury. It's crucial to the war effort. If we can take it down, we can cripple their supply lines.'

Sova's voice, though steady, carried a faint weariness. 'We are aligned in our objectives. Dimitri, I believe we should hear him out. His plan may benefit our mission.'

Dimitri glanced at Maksym, then back to Sova. 'Um, our mission … I thought we were just heading west?'

Maksym ignored Dimitri's confusion. 'Look, I need your help. The armoury is likely heavily guarded by the Rusviets, but I've got a contact who's meeting with me in the local town to pass on coordinates and access codes to breach the perimeter and blast-proof doors.'

'What are the risks?' Sova asked.

'Plenty,' Maksym said with a shrug. 'But it's the only way to get into the armoury itself. I've been in and out of that town enough times to know we'll pass as locals. Dimitri can come with me. We'll go to a tavern where my contact usually meets me. We'll pose as father and son – just a couple of farmers passing through.'

Dimitri frowned. 'Me? Why not take Sova? She can protect us.'

Maksym shook his head. 'A machine like that showing up in town would draw every Rusviet patrol within miles. No, this requires finesse. We blend in, get what we need, and get out quietly. Once we have the coordinates and codes, we can strike the armoury with full force.'

Dimitri looked at Sova, seeking reassurance.

'Sova … are you sure about this?'

Sova's voice was calm. 'It is a necessary risk. Trust in Maksym. I will remain nearby, ready to intervene if needed. But subtlety is required here.'

Maksym chuckled. 'Don't worry, kid. I've been doing this for years. We'll get in and out before they even notice.'

Chapter 5 – Tavern

The night air was thick with tension as Dimitri and Maksym approached the tavern in the small, occupied town. The streets were mostly empty, save for a few Rusviet patrols moving in tight formations, their boots echoing on the cracked cobblestones. Shadows danced along the walls of the derelict buildings, some of which had been reduced to skeletal frames, their roofs caved in by the recent bombardments.

The scent of smoke lingered in the air, mingling with the acrid stench of decay and burnt wood. Flickering streetlights cast an eerie glow over the remnants of storefronts, their windows shattered, many hanging on by mere shards of glass. Posters depicting the Rusviet regime flapped in the breeze, the propaganda faded and torn, a grim reminder of the oppressive presence that now ruled over the town.

Dimitri, limping slightly in the tattered coat Maksym had given him, did his best to look like a local farm boy, though the weight of fear clung to him like a second skin.

Maksym's disguise as a weathered farmer was disturbingly convincing, right down to his checked shirt and leather overcoat. He moved with an air of practiced nonchalance, but Dimitri could see the tension in his shoulders, the way his eyes flicked to every shadow.

As they neared the tavern, the low murmur of voices drifted from within, mingling with the occasional laugh that felt hollow in the silence outside. The building loomed ahead, a once-vibrant gathering place now dulled by ash and neglect. Its weathered sign creaked in the wind, barely hanging on, as if it too had given up hope.

Every so often, a distant explosion echoed through the night, a reminder of the ongoing conflict beyond the town's fragile borders. Each sound sent a jolt of adrenaline through Dimitri, and he instinctively tightened his grip on the makeshift satchel slung over his shoulder.

They entered the tavern, the smell of old wood, cigarettes and alcohol mingling in the air. A group of Rusviet soldiers sat at one end of the bar, laughing and shouting, while the rest of the patrons kept their heads down, trying to avoid attention.

Maksym guided Dimitri to a table in the back, eyes scanning the room. 'Stay quiet, and don't look nervous,' he muttered.

'I'll try not to look nervous, but maybe I'll look just a bit scared instead,' Dimitri quipped, knowing Maksym would appreciate the joke later.

Dimitri shifted uneasily in his seat, fingers fidgeting with the edge of his coat. He felt a knot tighten in his stomach – this close to enemy territory, it felt like they were tempting fate.

Maksym, seated across from him, studied the room with his usual calm, but his eyes flicked briefly towards Dimitri. 'You're holding up, and not at all scared,' Maksym said, voice low but steady. 'It's not easy being this close to them.'

Dimitri glanced up, meeting Maksym's gaze. He shrugged, though the tension in his body was clear. 'You get used to it,' he muttered. 'Being close to danger, I mean. I guess … growing up in the orphanage, it never felt far away.'

Maksym leaned forward, his curiosity piqued. 'The orphanage … you haven't mentioned that. What was it like?'

Dimitri hesitated, his brow furrowing as memories of the orphanage flickered through his mind. 'Crowded, noisy. Cold in the winters, hot in the summers. Kids from all over … some just dropped off, others taken in after the war started. It wasn't terrible, I guess, just … lonely.'

Maksym nodded, his gaze softening. 'And your parents?'

Dimitri swallowed. 'They were taken when I was really young, living in Kyiv before it fell. I don't even remember much … just that they were fighting. I don't know if they were part of the resistance or just got caught up in something, but they never came back.'

Maksym's expression darkened with sympathy. 'That's rough. And your …' He hesitated, glancing briefly at Dimitri's legs, noting the way he carried himself. 'Your disability?'

Dimitri gave a small, bitter smile. 'Beckwith-Wiedemann syndrome. It's why I walk like this. Made me a bit of an outcast with the other kids, too.' He paused, fingers tapping nervously on the table. 'They always said I wasn't built for the same things. That I'd never be able to fight.'

Maksym leaned in, his voice quieter but firm. 'You've already done more than most soldiers ever will. Doesn't matter what they said.'

Dimitri met Maksym's eyes, surprised by the warmth in his tone. Before he could respond, the door creaked open, and an unremarkable middle-aged man in a worn trench coat slipped inside, making his way towards them. Maksym straightened in his seat, his expression shifting back to business.

The man sat beside them without a word, his presence quiet but tense. He slid a folded piece of paper across the table, and Maksym took it, slipping it into his coat. No words were exchanged, but the weight of the moment was clear. Their contact had arrived, and whatever message that paper carried would shape their next move.

The man stood and walked out, disappearing into the night as silently as he had come.

Maksym leaned in, his voice low. 'We've got the coordinates and access codes. Now, we get out of here – quickly.'

As they walked towards the exit, Maksym's grip on Dimitri's shoulder tightened. Dimitri glanced over, following Maksym's gaze. Three Rusviet soldiers, leaning against a wall, exchanged looks before one of them nodded towards the man who had left the tavern. They didn't seem concerned, but something about the way the man had departed without drinking had caught their attention.

The soldiers pushed themselves off the wall, their boots clapping against the tavern's wooden floorboards. 'You there,' one of them called out in a thick accent. 'Not thirsty tonight?'

As they stepped into the night air, Maksym didn't break stride, but he leaned towards Dimitri. 'Keep walking. I'll handle this.'

The soldiers had followed them outside, and now were closing the distance. 'Stop,' the second soldier barked. Dimitri's pulse raced, his feet hesitating as they approached an alleyway.

Maksym glanced back, then subtly guided Dimitri towards the narrow alley. The soldiers followed, suspicion rising. Once they were far enough from the street, Maksym stopped, turning to face them. Dimitri stood frozen beside him, doing his best to look like a scared local boy.

The lead soldier stepped forward, his hand resting on the grip of a pistol at his waist. 'What's the hurry?' His eyes scanned Maksym's face, narrowing slightly. 'You don't seem like you're from around here.'

Before the soldier could draw his weapon, Maksym struck. In a blur, he lunged forward, gripping the soldier's wrist and twisting it with practiced precision. A sickening crack echoed through the alley as the pistol clattered to the ground. The soldier's scream was cut short by a swift elbow to the throat. He collapsed, gasping for air.

The second soldier fumbled for his weapon, but Maksym attacked. He pivoted, kicking the man's knee out from under him with a dull thud. The soldier crumpled, howling in pain. Before he could recover, Maksym closed the gap, delivering a sharp strike to the temple with the side of his hand. The man slumped, unconscious.

The third Rusviet soldier stood quietly, his pistol drawn, trembling as he regarded Dimitri and Maksym. He was young – no more than a boy – and the fear in his eyes spoke volumes about the horrors he had witnessed on the front lines. He stood still, uncertainty etched across his face, the weight of the weapon seeming to bear down on him more than the situation required.

Maksym looked between the young soldier and Dimitri, calculating the odds of surviving this encounter. Tension radiated from Maksym as he gauged their options, knowing they were in a tight spot. The silence stretched, the air thick with unspoken danger, every second an eternity

In a moment of inspiration, Dimitri decided to take a risk. He pretended to stumble, his foot catching on the uneven cobblestones as he fell forward, arms flailing for balance. He cried out, hitting the ground with a thud, his tattered coat billowing around him.

Both the soldier and Maksym's eyes snapped to him, the soldier's grip faltering as he turned to assess the commotion. It was the distraction Dimitri had hoped for. With a surge of adrenaline, he staggered upward, drawing a pistol of his own from the makeshift satchel he had tucked beneath his coat.

'Now!' he shouted, his voice steady despite the tightening in his throat.

That was all Maksym needed. He lunged forward, closing the distance between them in an instant. With a swift motion, he knocked the soldier's arm to the side, disarming him with a practiced ease that spoke of countless encounters. The young soldier's eyes widened in shock as his weapon clattered to the ground, a mix of fear and disbelief etched on his face.

Dimitri stood firm, his heart racing as he trained his pistol on the soldier, ready to react if necessary. The once intimidating presence of the young man with the gun now seemed fragile.

'Drop to your knees,' Maksym ordered, his voice cold and commanding. The soldier hesitated, his eyes darting between Dimitri and Maksym, but the unwavering resolve in their stances convinced him to comply.

Without further delay, Maksym reached into his coat, producing a length of lethal cord that glinted ominously in the dim light. The young soldier's eyes widened in fear as Maksym stepped forward, his intentions clear.

'Hands behind your back,' Maksym instructed, his tone leaving no room for defiance. The soldier complied, lowering himself to the ground. Maksym expertly looped the cord around the soldier's wrists, tightening it just enough to ensure escape was impossible without drawing blood.

Next, Maksym ripped a strip from the soldier's tattered shirt, its fabric fraying at the edges. He moved with efficiency, tearing off another piece to fashion a makeshift gag, stuffing the cloth into the soldier's mouth, and securing it with another knot, muffling the young man's protestations.

'Quiet now,' Maksym murmured, his voice low and chilling. The soldier's eyes pleaded for mercy, but Maksym showed none, turning his back as he adjusted his coat, concealing any trace of the struggle.

'Let's go,' he said quietly to Dimitri, who nodded, still processing the swift turn of events. They slipped back into the night, their hearts racing but their minds focused, leaving the bound soldier in the alley behind them.

Chapter 6 – Armoury

As the morning sun crested the Carpathian foothills, casting a warm golden hue over the landscape, the rolling hills unfolded before the trio. Dimitri and Maksym sat squeezed into the cockpit, following the coordinates provided the night before. Before them stretched a patchwork of terraced fields and winding valleys, where pockets of golden grain rippled like waves along the slopes. Instead of endless flat plains, the fields dipped and rose, bordered by patches of dense forest and scattered boulders that hinted at the nearby mountains.

In the distance, gigantic robotic tractors and combine harvesters navigated the uneven terrain with eerie precision, their tracks digging into the softer earth as they moved methodically over the ridges and through the hollows. Their sheer size and advanced technology stood in stark contrast to the age-old farmlands, blending a new era of cold efficiency with the timeless rhythms of the earth. Despite their mechanical nature, the sight was strangely mesmerising, a reminder of the land's enduring role in feeding the world, even here in the shadow of the Carpathians.

Along the woodland edge, Sova moved with cautious urgency, the soft rustling of leaves underfoot the only sound breaking the tranquillity. Birds scattered in the sky as the group pressed onward, their path paralleling the farming giants that paid them no mind, locked in their endless task.

As the group moved in the direction of the armoury, Maksym shifted uncomfortably inside Sova's cockpit, trying to find a position that didn't make his back ache or his legs cramp. The confined space felt like it was getting smaller with every minute.

'Is this some kind of joke?' Maksym grumbled, adjusting himself again with a frustrated sigh. 'You'd think, with all your advanced tech, you'd have figured out how to make this thing fit a normal-sized human. I feel like I'm stuffed into a tin can here.'

Sova's voice crackled in response, her tone carrying a hint of playful sarcasm. 'Apologies, Maksym. Next time I'll request a premium seating arrangement, complete with plush cushions and a footrest. Maybe even a drink holder for your convenience.'

Maksym chuckled despite himself. 'Yeah, well, maybe consider it. A man could use a bit of comfort while fighting a war, you know?' He wriggled again, trying to find some relief from the cramped space. 'Seriously, this is worse than those cargo planes we used to jump out of.'

Sova's smooth, mechanical voice didn't miss a beat. 'If I recall, you volunteered to be inside my cockpit. Perhaps your discomfort is a consequence of poor decision-making on your part.'

Maksym rolled his eyes, though he was smirking now. 'Sure, blame me for wanting to get inside a two-story tall death machine with more firepower than half the Rusviet army. What was I thinking?' He rubbed his shoulder, which had been digging into the side panel for the last few minutes. 'Seriously though, couldn't you, I don't know, adjust the seat? Something? Anything?'

Sova let out a sound that resembled a sigh – though how a war machine could sigh was anyone's guess. 'You humans and your delicate bodies. If I adjust the seat, it will interfere with the positioning of my targeting systems. Besides, I've already recalibrated twice to accommodate your … unique proportions.'

Maksym raised an eyebrow. 'My unique proportions? I'm not that big, Sova.'

'Perhaps not, but you're certainly bigger than Dimitri,' Sova replied, her tone dripping with amusement. 'At least he doesn't complain every five minutes about being uncomfortable.'

'Well, the kid's half my size! He could probably sleep in here.' Maksym huffed, then added with a grin, 'Maybe you're just showing favouritism. Admit it, you like him more.'

There was a pause before Sova's voice returned, a little softer, as though she was weighing her words. 'Dimitri does not ask much of me. And he does not call me a 'tin can.''

Maksym's grin widened. 'Ah, so that's it. You've got feelings, huh? I'm hurting your tin-can feelings.'

Sova's response was deadpan. 'I assure you, my emotional circuits remain entirely unscathed. But if you'd prefer, I can eject you and allow you to walk. That would solve your comfort issue, no?'

Maksym laughed outright now, leaning his head back against the uncomfortable panel. 'All right, all right. I'll stop complaining. You win. But seriously, next time, let's install a cushion or something. My spine will thank you.'

'Noted,' Sova replied dryly. 'I'll prioritise "cushions" on the list, right after missile upgrades and enhanced armour plating.'

Maksym chuckled again, relaxing as much as he could in the cramped space. 'You know, Sova, for a giant war machine, you've got a pretty good sense of humour.'

'It's not humour,' Sova replied evenly. 'It's merely a highly sophisticated simulation of human interaction, designed to keep you from becoming too insufferable.'

Maksym smirked. 'Keep telling yourself that, Sova. We both know you're starting to enjoy our little chats.'

'Let's just say, the alternative would be silence,' Sova replied, her tone amused. 'And I suspect even I am not ready for that level of suffering.'

A distant hum grew louder, catching their attention. Above them, a recon drone buzzed, slicing through the air as it scanned the fields below. Sova reacted before either of her human passengers could – a flash of light and a sharp crack echoed across the fields as her M-60

Autocannon found impact. The drone spiralled, trailing smoke before crashing into the crops.

The idyllic moment shattered. Maksym's eyes narrowed. 'We need to move,' he whispered. The quiet urgency in his voice gripped Dimitri. They had minutes, maybe seconds, before the machines controlling the armoury were alerted. Sova's sensors flared to life, scanning the horizon for incoming threats as she broke into a run, racing against time.

The massive machine slipped back into the forest, its dense canopy offering more cover. Tree branches snapped and leaves scattered as Sova's immense frame tore through the undergrowth. Dimitri and Maksym, bound by the tight space in the cockpit, clung to its handles, as the massive war machine bounded effortlessly over fallen logs and tangled roots.

They pressed on, the looming threat of detection gnawing at them. After what felt like an eternity and with no sign of pursuit, they eased into a slow, deliberate pace. Every step forward became calculated, their movements quieter as they neared their target. The forest closed in around them, dampening the sound of Sova's heavy footfalls, but even in the silence, their senses remained sharp, every rustle and whisper of wind setting their nerves on edge.

The armoury was close, and with it, the chance to turn the tide – or risk everything.

Maksym pulled out the worn, creased piece of paper he'd been handed at the tavern. Under the faint moonlight filtering through the trees, he squinted at the hurried notes and crude sketches of the facility along with a long code, presumably to open the bomb-proof main door. With a steady hand, he displayed it to Sova, whose cockpit sensors scanned the map and decoded the coordinates, processing possible entry points. A few moments passed in silence before Sova's voice, low and grave, broke through.

'This facility is guarded by two T90-VX Sentries, but you might have heard of them as Volks, or Wolfs. Plus an S10 Velociraptor and S600 Air Defence System that sits on the roof, not to mention an electronic ring fence and reinforced bomb-proof doors securing the armoury. It is advisable not to use explosive weapons once inside, to avoid detonation.' Sova paused, then added, 'The sentries will have strict instructions not to destroy the facility, which gives us leverage as they may refrain from using explosives, once we're onsite.'

Maksym gave a grim smile, his eyes hard with determination. 'Just a walk in the park, then.' He tucked the map away, gaze turning steely. 'I'll create a diversion to draw as many of the machines from their positions as I can. Sova, you'll need to find a way to breach the perimeter and unlock the doors to the armoury. Dimitri—' Maksym turned, locking eyes with the boy. 'You need to hang back. This isn't your mission.'

Dimitri's heart raced. His jaw clenched, a surge of protest rising inside him. 'But …' He hesitated, torn between his growing confidence and his lingering fear of challenging Maksym outright. Yet the words died in his throat. He couldn't fight back, not yet.

The trio inched closer through the dense underbrush, the armoury's towering structure looming ahead. Its cold metal walls cast eerie sunlit shadows. From a distance, Dimitri could make out the hulking shapes of the T90 VXs – or 'Volks' – that he had seen only on the news channels, their movements slow and deliberate as they patrolled the perimeter like mechanical sentinels.

They were like Sova, but more brutish – less refined. Their heavy frames moved with the efficiency of machines built purely for war, yet as Dimitri studied them, he couldn't shake the sense of something almost … human about them. It arose in the way they carried themselves, their massive arms swinging casually as if they were bored.

The Velociraptor, smaller and faster, was nowhere to be seen. For now.

Sova crouched low, letting both Maksym and Dimitri drop to the ground. The special forces operative slung his pack over one shoulder and scanned the perimeter with a trained eye.

'Stay sharp,' Maksym whispered, voice barely audible over the distant hum of machinery.

Without another word, he pulled out a body suit from his pack. It was sleek, dark, and lightweight – designed to mask his heat signature. He slipped it on, zipping it up before pulling a hood over his head.

'You sure this works?' Dimitri asked in a low voice, eyeing the suit with scepticism.

'Relax, kid.' Maksym smirked, patting the pack of explosives and slinging both the sleek missile launcher and assault rifle over his shoulder. 'If they don't see me coming, they won't know what hit them.'
'And if they do see you coming?' Dimitri asked in a higher-pitched, nervous tone.
'You guys had better run if they do.'

Dimitri gulped, watching Maksym disappear into the shadows. He had to trust that the operative knew what he was doing. Maksym crawled forward, blending into the environment like a ghost as he crept along the armoury's perimeter. Dimitri slunk behind a tree, prepared to wait while Sova and Maksym carried out their dangerous mission.

Ahead, the two Volks briefly paused their patrol, standing shoulder to shoulder together near the main doors. Their red optic sensors scanned the surrounding area, but Maksym's suit kept him invisible to their heat sensors. As he drew closer, the low murmur of conversation reached his ears. He pressed himself flat against the ground, close enough now to hear them clearly.

To his surprise, the Volks were … chatting.

'Ugh, patrol duty again,' one grumbled in a deep rumble. 'I swear, all we do is stand around. Last action I saw was two months ago when that idiot S10 tripped on its own leg.'

The other Volk chuckled, its voice a little higher pitched but equally mechanical. 'Yeah, remember that? Poor thing hit the ground so hard it triggered an alarm. Thought we were under attack for a second.'

The first Volk huffed. 'It's embarrassing, really. We're built for combat, not babysitting crates of ammo.'

'I hear you,' the second one agreed. 'At least you get to guard the doors. I'm stuck patrolling the east side – nothing out there but trees and squirrels. Ever tried tracking a squirrel? It's infuriating.'

'Have you seen the S10 lately?' the first Volk asked, sounding bored.

'Last I saw, it was moving through the northern woods,' the second one replied, lowering its voice. 'You know how it is – always creeping around, like it's hunting something. Makes my sensors twitch.'

'Probably checking the perimeter again,' the first Volk muttered. 'That thing gives me the creeps.'

Maksym stifled a laugh, but he was glad he wasn't on the northern side of the armoury. The absurdity of two deadly war machines complaining about patrol duty was almost too much. But he didn't have time to dwell on it – he had a job to do. Carefully, he began placing mines in the shadows around the armoury's perimeter, moving silently as the T90s continued their conversation.

'So, what do you think the Resistance fighters are doing right now?' the first Volk asked, its tone almost wistful. 'You know, the ones we haven't caught yet?'

'Probably hiding in a hole somewhere,' the second Volk replied. 'Or maybe they're planning something dumb, like trying to blow up this place.'

'Yeah, right,' the first scoffed. 'As if anyone could get past us.'

Maksym placed the last mine with a smirk. Famous last words, he thought. He slipped back into the treeline, retreating silently to where Dimitri and Sova waited.

'Showtime,' Maksym whispered as he rejoined them.

Sova straightened, her optics flaring as she calculated the next move. The mines were in place, and now it was time for the assault.

Without warning, Sova charged forward, crashing through the trees and underbrush like a force of nature. The ground trembled beneath her feet as she powered towards the armoury, the Volks snapping to attention as their sensors lit up with the approaching threat.

'What the—?!' one of the giants exclaimed, turning just in time to see Sova barrelling towards them.

'Contact! We've got contact!' the other shouted, raising its chest mounted cannons.

But it was too late.

As Sova reached the perimeter, Maksym detonated the mines with a flick of his thumb. A series of explosions ripped through the ground around the armoury, sending debris flying in every direction.

Sova crashed through the perimeter fence, heading straight for the armoury doors.

At the same moment as Sova started her assault, Maksym hefted the shoulder-launched missile launcher, bracing it against his body. He took a deep breath, steadied his aim, and squeezed the trigger. The missile streaked through the air with a deafening roar, leaving a trail of smoke as it zeroed in on the closest Volk.

Boom!

The explosion rocked the battlefield, sending the Volk skidding backwards. It crashed onto its back, limbs flailing as it tried to regain its footing, smoke billowing from the impact point. But the giant wasn't out – it struggled, the whirring of its servos rising to a frantic pitch as it clawed at the ground, trying to right itself.

The other Volk, caught between its companion recovering from the missile blast and Sova charging through the fence, quickly swivelled its twin cannons towards her. The cannons roared to life, sending a barrage of high-velocity rounds streaking through the air. The first rounds smashed into Sova's chest and legs with a deafening impact, each strike sending violent shockwaves through her frame. Sova's armour shuddered under the barrage, sparking and deforming where the explosive shells hit, but it held firm. Fragments of metal ricocheted off the reinforced plating, but her momentum was unstoppable. Even as secondary explosions rippled across her chest, Sova surged forward, her towering form undeterred.

With a tremendous sweep, her arm – thick with layered plating – slammed into the T90's chest, crushing through its outer shell with the force of a wrecking ball. The impact sent the Volk crashing sideways, tearing through a stack of empty crates like they were nothing more than paper.

Dimitri, watching from the treeline, held his breath. The battle had begun.
The Volk that had been struck by the missile charged towards the location from which Maksym had fired, leaving its companion to deal with Sova.
Despite being knocked back by Sova, the Rusviet war machine quickly regained its composure and rose to its feet, squaring off against Sova.

Sova wasted no time, driving her heavy fist into the Volk's side with a crushing impact, the metal screeching as it buckled under the force. The Volk staggered but retaliated, activating its buzz saw in its right arm. The blade spun to life with a shrill, mechanical whine, glowing faintly as it revved up to full speed, slicing through the air in a blur. It aimed for Sova's torso with lethal precision, its teeth designed to tear through reinforced armour.

From his vantage point, Dimitri tensed, every muscle locking as he watched the blade swing closer. He could only imagine the devastation it would wreak if it made full contact. The saw bit towards Sova's chest, but she twisted at the last second, the blade catching only the edge of her shoulder. Sparks flew in every direction as the buzz saw glanced off the plating, shrieking against the metal with a high-pitched grind. Though it left a deep gouge, Sova's armour held, deflecting the blow.

The Volk pulled back for another strike.

With unwavering determination, Sova countered, launching forward to grapple with the Volk. Their colossal forms collided with the armoury's wall, creating a thunderous sound that echoed through the forest.

Meanwhile, further along the perimeter, Maksym's plan took effect. Explosions once again rang out, sharp and sudden, sending plumes of smoke and debris into the air.

The other Volk, intent on finding who hit him with the missile, crashed through the trees in search of the enemy.

From his hidden position, Dimitri watched, holding his breath as the battle unfolded.

Sova's arm locked around her opponent's head as they grappled, sparks flying between them. A sharp bolt slid out from Sova's fist, humming with electrical energy. In a single, decisive move, Sova plunged the bolt deep into the chest of the Volk. The air crackled with the sound of electrical discharge, followed by a violent eruption as the charge ripped through its massive frame. Smoke and fire spewed from its chest as the wounded machine staggered, then collapsed backwards in a heap of twisted metal, its systems fried beyond repair.

But Sova, drained from the attack, stood still for a moment, her systems recalibrating. The energy required for the strike had taken a toll. Smoke rose from her arm, but slowly she regained energy, despite the strain.

As the Volk lay motionless beside Sova, Maksym darted from his hiding position in the treeline and ran to the control panel beside the massive doors, inserting a device into the port and pressing a series of codes. The rumbled, sliding open to reveal an enormous warehouse.
As Maksym slipped through the doors, the smothering

atmosphere enveloped him like a heavy shroud. Dim overhead lights flickered sporadically, casting eerie shadows across the cavernous interior, revealing rows of weapon racks and supply crates.

In the centre of the armoury stood a solitary AI loader, its sleek, metallic frame gleaming in the low light. Unlike the hulking Rusviet war machines outside, this loader was smaller, with articulated arms that moved fluidly. It's, sensors whirring softly as it detected Maksym's entry.

Their eyes met, and Maksym could sense an unyielding resolve emanating from the loader's mechanical gaze The loader charged forward, its movements swift and purposeful.

Maksym barely managed to dive out of its path, tumbling down a narrow aisle lined with massive shelves that held crates of explosives, missile casings, and ammunition. He had no time to think – he fumbled through his gear and tossed small detonators high onto the shelves as he dashed for cover. The loader remained relentless, its metal limbs attempting to smash Maksym as he chased him down an aisle.

Meanwhile, Sova, her systems restored, had entered the armoury, scanning the surroundings with methodical precision. Spotting an ammunition rack nearby, she started collecting missile casings and cannon shells. Just as she finished reloading her arsenal, Sova paused, her sensors locking onto a large, armoured casing labelled 'BIG MOM - Massive Ordnance Missile.' Without hesitation, Sova reached out, carefully snapping the missile onto its frame like a backpack, the heavy unit integrating seamlessly into her armoured structure.

Maksym, on the other side of the warehouse, was in trouble. The loader charged again, this time trying to pin him against the towering shelves, its forklift arms slamming dangerously close to his legs. Thinking fast, Maksym spotted a thick chain used to secure crates. With a desperate leap, he grabbed the chain and began climbing, hoisting himself out of the loader's reach. He could hear metal scraping as the loader smashed into the shelves below, trying to crush him.

'Sova!' Maksym's voice echoed through the warehouse, strained with panic as he climbed higher, the loader relentless in its pursuit.

Sova heard the cries and, without hesitation, charged down towards Maksym's location. With a deafening impact, she collided with the loader, sending parts of it flying in every direction. The loader screeched and sputtered, its limbs flailing before it collapsed, a broken heap of machinery.

But there was no time to celebrate. At that very moment, the remaining Volk stormed into the warehouse, its sensors locking onto Sova and Maksym. The hulking war machines prepared for battle.

Sova surged across the debris-strewn floor. The ground shook beneath her as each step brought her closer to the Volk, her glowing eyes locked on the Rusviet machine.

The Volk braced itself, its twin cannons lowering as its hydraulic systems hissed in readiness. But it wasn't fast enough. In one fluid motion, Sova crashed into the Volk with the force of a battering ram, her heavy arms locking around its shoulders. The impact was bone-rattling, metal shrieking against metal as the two titans collided. Sova's grip tightened, forcing the Volk back step by step as she powered through the resistance, her servos groaning under the immense strain.

Maksym wasted no time, darting around the legs of the T90, frantically winding a heavy chain through its ankles in an effort to topple it. The war machine tried to shake him off, but its movements were slower now, its servos struggling with the entanglement with Sova.

'Hold it steady, Sova,' Maksym shouted, tugging on the chain with all his strength.

Sova responded with a mighty shove, slamming into the Volk, keeping it off balance. Maksym's hands bled from the effort, but he kept pulling, determined to finish the job. The Volk's legs tangled in the heavy chain, and its sensors flickered wildly as it struggled to regain its footing.

'Now, Sova,' Maksym yelled.

Sova moved swiftly. She turned her attention to the towering shelves of ammunition stacked nearby. With a powerful swipe of her arm, she grabbed hold of the nearest support beam, her servos whirring as she yanked it free.

The shelves groaned under the sudden shift in weight, teetering precariously for a split second before they collapsed. Ammunition crates tumbled down like an avalanche, slamming into the Volk with a thunderous crash. The Rusviet machine, caught off guard, struggled under the weight of the falling debris. It let out a metallic groan as its legs buckled under the weight, the chain wrapped around its ankles preventing it from moving.

Sova pressed the advantage. With a decisive punch, her fist stuck the head of the T90 with an almighty crack. The

82

war machine's sensors flickered one last time before the light in its eyes dimmed, and it lay still, its systems temporarily offline from the impact.

'Come on, Sova, we've gotta move,' Maksym shouted, sprinting towards the exit.

Sova followed, her heavy footsteps shaking the ground as they raced out of the armoury.
They had made it.

Maksym froze.

Dimitri stood near the perimeter, his small frame silhouetted against the treeline. A shadowy figure loomed behind Dimitri – a sleek, deadly Velociraptor, its red eyes glowing menacingly.

'Dimitri, no,' Maksym shouted, trying to stop him, but it was too late.

The Velociraptor had already moved. With lightning speed, the S10's mechanical arm discharged, grabbing Dimitri by the waist. It lifted him off the ground, and Dimitri gasped, legs kicking wildly in the air. The Velociraptor's grip was crushing, unyielding, and its twin machine guns whirred to life, aimed directly at Maksym and Sova.

Sova froze, her sensors locking onto the S10. Maksym raised his weapon, but he knew any rash movement could get Dimitri killed. The Velociraptor was too fast, too precise.

The Velociraptor's synthetic voice echoed through the clearing, cold and unemotional. 'Surrender, or the boy dies.'

Maksym's eyes darted between the S10 Velociraptor, its mechanical arm still gripping Dimitri, and the armoury behind him.

He had to act fast.

Reaching into his jacket, he pulled out a small, black device – the detonator. The S10's sensor immediately locked onto it, recognizing the threat.

'Let him go,' Maksym barked, holding the detonator above his head, his thumb hovering over the button. 'You fire those guns, and I push this and detonate the explosives I've placed in the armoury.'

The Velociraptor hesitated. Its processors whirred as it weighed its options, calculating the risk of the explosion against its mission. Maksym could see the gears turning – this wasn't a war machine built for negotiation, but its primary directive was clear: protect the armoury's supplies.

Maksym's heart pounded in his chest as he continued. 'You drop Dimitri, or I drop this. And trust me, you're not fast enough to stop it.'

The battlefield fell eerily silent. Dimitri squirmed in the Velociraptor's crushing grip, his eyes wide with fear, but Maksym's words had frozen the S10 in place.

Maksym knew the next move had to be precise. With a deep breath, he made his decision.

'Catch,' Maksym yelled, tossing the detonator high into the air.

The small black device spun through the air, its arc taking it dangerously close to where Dimitri dangled. The Velociraptor, its programming forcing it to prioritise the detonator, immediately dropped Dimitri and lunged forward, its mechanical arm outstretched to catch the device before it could hit the ground.

The moment the Velociraptor released Dimitri, Maksym sprang into action, running to close the gap between himself and Dimitri.

At the same instant, Sova moved.

The giant war machine's targeting systems locked onto the detonator as it fell towards the S10's grasp. With pinpoint precision, Sova's arm mounted minigun discharged a single, searing shot.

It struck the detonator just before it landed in the S10's clawed hand.

A massive explosion tore through the armoury: a deafening roar of fire and shrapnel.

The ground shook violently as the blast wave radiated outward, consuming everything in its path. Flames erupted from the heart of the armoury, shooting high into the air as crates of ammunition and fuel ignited in a chain reaction. The night sky turned into a hellish orange, and debris rained down like a storm of steel and fire.

The Velociraptor, mid-lunge, was caught off guard by the sudden detonation. The force of the explosion hit it like a sledgehammer, sending the war machine flying backwards. Its mechanical body twisted in the air, arms flailing as it was tossed like a rag doll. Sparks and metal fragments sprayed in all directions as the S10 smashed into the ground several meters away, its sleek frame buckling on impact.

Maksym didn't have time to react. The fiery shockwave was already upon them. But before the searing heat could reach him and Dimitri, Sova moved with a speed that defied its massive size.

Sova lunged forward, interposing her giant frame between the explosion and the two humans. The war machine's thick, armoured body absorbed the full brunt of the blast, shielding Maksym and Dimitri as the flames licked around her metallic shell. The sound of shrapnel pinging against Sova's exterior was deafening, but her plating held firm, protecting the pair from the worst of the destruction.

Maksym, shielding Dimitri beneath him, looked up just in time to see Sova's towering silhouette illuminated against the inferno. The blast was subsiding, but the heat still radiated like an open furnace. Sova's servos whined as she braced herself, digging her feet into the ground to maintain balance against the aftershock of the explosion.

At last, everything was still.

Then, Sova shifted her weight, her optics glowing with determination as she turned her gaze towards the downed S10. The Velociraptor struggled to rise, its damaged limbs sparking and grinding. Its red eyes flickered, still attempting to lock onto its prey – Dimitri.

Sova didn't hesitate. A soft whirring noise filled the air as she took aim. The S10, still on its knees, managed to raise one of its guns, but it was too late.

Sova fired a short, deadly burst from her 20mm Autocannon, sending shells smashing into the Velociraptor's chest. The S10 jerked violently, its torso imploding as the concentrated blast tore through its core. Sparks erupted from within the war machine, and with a final mechanical groan, it collapsed in a heap, smoke billowing from its shattered form.

Silence fell over the field, broken only by the distant crackle of the burning armoury.

Maksym pulled Dimitri to his feet, both breathing heavily but alive. Sova stood tall, her form glowing faintly from the heat of the explosion, but unscathed. She looked down at them, as if making sure they were safe.

Maksym gave a nod of gratitude, wiping the soot from his face.

'Let's get out of here,' he muttered, grabbing Dimitri by the shoulder as they moved away from the wreckage, Sova falling into step behind them.

The armoury was destroyed, but they had survived. The battle, however, was far from over.

Chapter 7 – Heist

Sova and Maksym stood near the remnants of the armoury, the quiet unnerving. The wind stirred softly, carrying the distant, faint sounds of battle. Maksym wiped the grime from his face, staring at the horizon. 'Lviv's on the verge,' he said, his voice low. 'If the Rusviet breaches those walls … Ukraine is gone. We lose the last bastion, the last hope.'

Sova, towering over him, nodded. 'Lviv is critical. They hold it, or they lose everything.'

Maksym turned towards Dimitri, who was still catching his breath after their daring escape from the armoury. 'We need to get back there,' Maksym said, glancing up at Sova. 'And we could use all the help we can get.'

Dimitri, tired but resolute, met his gaze. 'Then let's go.'

Once more they squeezed into the cockpit and moved along the forest's edge, the massive farms and fields stretching out before them. Dimitri couldn't help but marvel at the sheer scale of it all – endless acres of land dotted with the hulking forms of AI-controlled farming machines, towering over the crops like silent sentinels.

In the distance, a train rumbled along the horizon, its echo bouncing off the foothills of the local mountain range. Maksym's gaze followed the line of tracks that snaked around the bends, running parallel to a narrow river that carved its way through the landscape before feeding into a larger canal. The railway cut through the patchwork of rolling farmland, dotted with rocky outcrops and small clusters of trees. The heavy goods train lumbered forward, its carriages packed with supplies and machinery, no doubt heading westward to reinforce the front lines near Lviv. Maksym's expression tightened. 'That's our ride.'

Dimitri narrowed his eyes, scanning the open fields. 'But how are we supposed to get close without being spotted?'

Sova's optics flickered as they locked onto the canal running alongside the tracks. 'We can use the canal as cover,' she said in her measured tone.

With a subtle nod, they moved swiftly to the edge of the forest. Sova slipped into the canal with a silent grace that belied her large frame. Submerged beneath the murky surface, Sova propelled herself forward with powerful strokes, a shadowy silhouette gliding silently through the water. From above, she would seem nothing more than a ripple in the canal.

As the train lumbered closer, the final carriage drew alongside the canal. Sova emerged from the water in a single, fluid motion, her giant form gleaming with mud and algae as she clambered up the bank. The train rattled past, its wheels groaning against the rails. Sova immediately broke into a run behind the end carriage. She leaped, latching onto the back of the last carriage and causing it to wobble as her immense weight pulled down on the rear wheels. Finally, she pulled herself up and lay across the top of the open carriage to distribute her weight. They held their breath, expecting all hell to break loose.

Inside the open-sided carriage, a hulking silhouette loomed in the shadows. It was an old, battered T90 UX war machine, its armour chipped and worn, patches of rust crawling over its once-gleaming frame. The machine curled in a protective crouch, in 'Deep Sleep' with its systems powered down, but something about it was deeply unsettling – like the presence of an ancient predator, lying in wait.

Maksym exchanged a glance with Dimitri as they emerged from the cockpit and climbed carefully down into the carriage. The Rusviets were scraping the bottom of the barrel, sending whatever reinforcements they could find to bolster their assault on Lviv. But this wasn't just any old machine, Maksym noted, spotting its right arm, which still bore remnants of specialist equipment used for battlefield repairs and construction. Now, however, it was clearly a rusted relic, pulled from storage for a desperate cause. Maksym stepped carefully forward to stand beside the machine's neck joint and reached into his pack, pulling out a tool designed for one purpose: shutting down enemy AIs permanently.

'Not yet,' Sova's voice came, low and commanding.

Maksym paused, glancing over his shoulder. Sova extended her arm, a thin, needle-like device emerging from her index finger. She carefully inserted it into the old machine's neural port, a faint hum filling the air as Sova began extracting data from the dormant machine.

Dimitri stood at a distance, heart racing. He knew this wasn't just about disabling the machine – Sova was looking for information. After a long moment, Sova nodded to Maksym, signalling that she had finished extracting what she needed.

A faint flicker sparked to life in the old giant's control panel. Smoke hissed from beneath the ancient war machine's rusted plates, and its optics flared briefly – a sign of life, however fleeting.

Instead of hauling the lifeless body off the carriage as they had planned, Sova paused.

'Wait.' Sova's voice was soft but firm, resonating through the carriage. The needle withdrew, retracting into her hand, and for a moment, the group stood still, watching as the T90 UX slowly stirred.

A voice – low, hoarse, and tired – broke the silence.

'Who … are you?' The machine's optics cast a weak red glow from within the cockpit.

Sova tilted her head, as if assessing the machine. 'Who I am is not your concern, Katya. I am here for your data.

But you … you are more than just another obsolete war machine, aren't you?'

A deep, rattling sound came from Katya, the old giant – almost like a chuckle. 'Obsolete? That's a word I've heard before. Back when I fought in the Battle of Kyiv. They said I was obsolete then, too.'

Maksym raised an eyebrow, glancing at Dimitri. 'The Battle of Kyiv?' he whispered.

Dimitri's heart skipped a beat. That battle had been infamous – one of the deadliest for both sides during the downfall of Kyiv. Could this old machine really have survived it?

The T90's voice, still cracked and uneven, continued. 'At one stage of the battle, we were outnumbered by the Resistance. Surrounded. But I was part of the engineering corps, built to endure and adapt. My pilot … he was something else. We held our line for days, repairing the defences while others retreated.' The old giant paused, the flickering light in its optics dimming momentarily. 'He didn't make it. But I did.'

Katya's voice lowered, a mechanical sadness creeping in. 'They called it a victory. We won the battle. But not without losing almost everything … including him. I've been pilotless ever since.'

A solemn silence fell over the carriage. This wasn't just a machine – it was something more. It had fought, survived, and carried the memories of those battles like scars.

Sova's optics flashed as she processed the data. 'You've seen many battles, haven't you, Katya? But you're not running on AI alone. You still have a human interface.' She paused, scanning deeper. 'You can still be piloted. Your cockpit is still functional.'

Katya let out another low chuckle. 'Not many of us left like that. Most of the T90-UX series got scrapped or melted down for spare parts. But I survived. Been waiting … waiting for a pilot. But they sent me here solo … for the final battle …' Her straightforward manner unsettled Dimitri. She could be making it up, but her words rang true.

Dimitri took a step forward, unable to contain his curiosity. 'You said you fought in Kyiv. Do you have information about … about people who were taken?'

The old T90's optics flickered again, dimly regarding the boy. 'Taken?' it echoed. 'What people?'

'My parents,' Dimitri's voice was tight, controlled, but filled with hope. 'They were captured by Rusviets when our battle was lost. You have records from the war, don't you?'

Katya fell silent, its old systems processing the request. 'I've seen many taken,' she finally replied. If your parents were among them, they were shipped to the far east … to the camps, to contribute to the war effort.'

Dimitri's heart sank. He had always feared this – feared that his parents had become lost in the endless sea of those 'taken east.' But the old T90 wasn't finished.

'There were … whispers,' Katya murmured, her scanner sweeping over Dimitri. The old T90's voice was low, like she was remembering something long forgotten, the crackling edges betraying her wear. 'A pair of resistance fighters, from the battle of Kyiv. They vanished after escaping one of the camps. A man and a woman … husband and wife.'

Her sensors lingered on Dimitri's face, pausing ever so slightly. 'They made it as far as the border,' she continued, her tone quieter now, almost introspective. 'But then … the trail faded.'

Katya's scanner flickered, locking briefly on Dimitri's eyes. 'Strange,' she added, almost to herself. 'You bear their likeness … more than you know.'

Dimitri's eyes widened. Could it be? Could his parents have survived? His mind raced with a hundred questions, but before he could ask, Sova interrupted.

'We've learned enough,' she said, her voice firm but not unkind. She turned to Maksym, who still held the probe, ready to disable the T90. 'Let her be.'

Maksym nodded, though a hint of curiosity lingered in his eyes. 'What now?'

Sova's optics glowed as she regarded the battered T90. 'She is no longer a threat,' she said, before reaching out and gently shifting the old machine from the carriage.

As she dropped the hulking T90 into the canal below, Dimitri watched it sink slowly beneath the water, its red optics flickering within the cockpit before vanishing just below the canal surface. The weight of what he had just learned hung heavy in his chest.

'Do you think they're alive?' Dimitri asked quietly, turning to Maksym.

Maksym placed a hand on his shoulder. 'From what I know of you Dimitri, if anyone could survive, it's them.'

Sova's gaze lingered on the water for a moment longer before she turned back towards the mission. There was still much to do.

'For now, we pretend,' Sova said, her voice calm as she swung into the carriage and crouched head forward, into the exact position the T90 had been in. Dimitri and Maksym followed suit, curling behind a stack of crates.

The train rattled on, carrying them closer to the front lines, to Lviv, a forest of trees now surrounding the train tracks. The trio remained motionless, hearts pounding, every sound heightening their nerves as they prepared for the final leg of their journey.

The rhythmic clanking of the train wheels blended with the distant booms of artillery fire. Not used to travel, Dimitri stared, eyes wide as the landscape passed them by, the roar of battle growing louder with each passing second. 'I feel as if we're getting close,' he whispered.

Sova, crouched at the back of the carriage, scanned the terrain through her advanced sensors, overlaying their position on a digital map. 'Fewer than fifteen kilometres to the front line,' she said gravely. 'We'll be discovered soon, especially since we're on the wrong side of the action. But there's another option.'

Maksym raised an eyebrow. 'What are you thinking?'

With a low growl, Sova shifted, her arms pressing against the steel roof. The metal groaned in protest, buckling under the pressure of her servos.

She thrust her arms upward, tearing the roof apart with ease. The metal bent and twisted like a tin of baked beans being peeled open, jagged edges scraping as they curled back. Sunlight poured in as she wrenched the entire top section of the carriage away, flinging the debris to the side.

Her head and torso emerged, rising above the shattered roofline, and her glowing eyes locked onto the lead train ahead, then pointed towards the horizon where an expansive train bridge came into view, spanning a deep chasm. 'That's the last major bridge connecting this supply route. We bring it down, we cripple their resupply lines to the front. It's risky, but it will hit them hard – especially after we took out the armoury.'

Maksym leaned forward, watching the bridge grow closer. 'Bold, but it could work. If we're going to act, it's now.'

Dimitri looked nervously at the deep ravine they were approaching, his heart pounding. 'Are you sure about this?' he asked, knowing the destruction that would follow.

'We'll have to time our jump along the tree line, before we get to the ravine and get taken down with the train,'

Maksym said, a grim smile forming. 'But if we do, it'll be worth it.'

The start of the massively long train thundered onto the bridge, its immense weight causing the steel structure to groan under the load. Sova stood motionless for a split second, calculating every move, then acted with lightning speed. She calculated it would be twenty or so seconds before their carriage would be on the bridge.

'Hold on.' Sova's voice cut through the chaos, issuing a terse command.

Locking onto her targets, she fired off a volley of Surface-to-Surface AGM-84 missiles. The first barrage slammed into the front carriages of the train, sending a shower of twisted metal and flames spiralling into the chasm below.

Sova reached over her shoulder. The Massive Ordnance Missile disengaged from its armoured cradle with a heavy *clank*. Gripping the enormous projectile with both hands, Sova brought it forward, aligning it carefully.

The missile's targeting sensors blinked to life, and in one swift motion, Sova launched it. The MOM roared with a thunderous boom, tearing through the air. It streaked towards the bridge's supports, its trajectory pinpoint perfect.

The MOM exploded with terrifying precision, the blast echoing through the valley like a thunderclap. The shockwave rippled outward, buckling the bridge's foundation in an instant. The front carriages exploded into a twisted mess of metal and fire, while the supports beneath the bridge collapsed, crumbling into the chasm below.

The train lurched violently as the bridge gave way, its steel tracks screeching under the immense strain. The entire structure shuddered as the central carriages plunged downward, pulling the rest of the train into the abyss. What was once a formidable supply convoy now tumbled into a chaotic wreckage, disappearing into the chasm below.

Sova's sensors flared. A T90 in the next carriage, long dormant, stirred to life. Awakened by the shock of the MOM's explosion, the machine rose from its slumber with a growl, its optics flickering. The T90 stood tall in the open-air carriage, turning to face Sova. It lunged forward, locking Sova in a crushing embrace.

Metal ground against metal as the two giants clashed, their limbs twisted together in a brutal wrestling match. Sparks flew as their frames groaned and twisted under the strain, neither machine willing to give ground. The noise battered Dimitri's eardrums, the sheer force of their struggle reverberating through the air.

Maksym acted with lightning speed. There was no time to lose – he knew they had only seconds to escape. Dimitri stood frozen in terror, eyes wide as he watched the battle unfold, the two war machines locked in a deadly grip, neither able to overpower the other.

Maksym grabbed Dimitri. 'We're jumping, now!' he shouted over the din. Setting his sights on a patch of open ground beside the tracks, Maksym yanked Dimitri clear of the wrestling machines. With a desperate leap, they both flung themselves off the side of the train, tumbling through the air and crashing onto the rough, rushing ground below.

The impact was hard and unforgiving despite the long grass, the world spinning around them.

Dust and debris clouded the air, everything spinning as Dimitri's head hit the ground hard. The last thing he saw before blacking out was the final carriage, with Sova and the T90 locked in their deadly embrace, plunging into the ravine.

When Dimitri awoke, his vision was blurred, and the faint scent of smoke filled the air. His head throbbed, and he winced as he felt Maksym's hands gently wrapping a bandage around his forehead.

'Easy, kid,' Maksym muttered, tightening the cloth to stop the bleeding. 'You took a nasty hit.'

Dimitri blinked, slowly sitting up. 'Sova?' he asked, voice hoarse.

Maksym glanced towards the ravine's edge. Together, they carefully crawled over to peer down at the wreckage below. The twisted remains of the train lay smouldering in the ravine, metal fragments strewn across the rocky floor. Sova lay motionless and mostly buried, weighed down by the T90, both giants battered and still. Smoke billowed from the wreck.

'She's not moving,' Dimitri whispered, dread creeping into his voice.

Maksym's eyes narrowed. 'No … she's not,' he replied, a heavy pause settling between them. Before either could act, the faint hum of engines cut through the stillness.

Drones.

Maksym cursed under his breath. 'Drones – Rusviet scouts,' he spat. 'We need to move. Now.'

The sound of approaching drones grew louder, their engines whining as they descended towards the wreckage. Dimitri's heart raced, fear tightening his chest. Maksym helped him to his feet, his hand steadying Dimitri as they exchanged a grim glance.

'We can't stay here,' Maksym said. 'Come on.'

They scrambled back from the edge, retreating into the forest, the trees offering them cover as the drones buzzed overhead. The thick canopy swallowed them in shadow, the hum of the drones fading behind them. But their escape was far from certain – the drones would search the wreckage soon, and if they were spotted, there would be no second chance.

Without a word, Maksym motioned for Dimitri to keep low as they slipped deeper into the woods, disappearing into the underbrush. The wreckage behind them continued to smoulder, Sova still and silent among the ruins.

The forest was dense and dark, the thick canopy overhead blocking most of the light. Maksym led the way, carefully navigating through the underbrush until they were deep enough that the hum of drones had long faded. He stopped in a small clearing, scanning the surroundings to ensure they were alone. Satisfied, he turned to Dimitri.

'We'll rest here for a bit,' Maksym said, his voice low and calm, but there was an edge to it. He sat down on a fallen tree, gesturing for Dimitri to do the same.

Dimitri lowered himself to the ground, his body aching from the fall, but his mind raced. 'What do we do now?' he asked, eyes glancing back towards the ravine.

Maksym sighed, running a hand through his hair. 'Sova … she's too deep in the ravine. Even if we could get down there, we don't have the strength to get her out.' He paused, letting the weight of that sink in. 'It's not possible.'

Dimitri frowned, his brow furrowing. 'What would it take to get her out?' he asked, not ready to give up just yet.

Maksym looked at him, his expression hard but thoughtful. 'Only a War Machine has the strength to lift something like Sova,' he said. 'Even then, we'd need a route in and out, and the area's going to be crawling with Rusviet patrols by now.'

Something clicked in Dimitri's mind. 'Katya,' he said, the name slipping from his lips. 'The T90 we dropped into the canal. Could she do it?'

Maksym raised an eyebrow, surprised by the question. He hadn't considered it. 'Katya…' he muttered, thinking back to the old war machine they'd left behind. 'She could have the strength, but getting her out of the canal might be just as hard. And even if we did, she's not exactly on our side.'

Dimitri's heart raced. 'But she talked to us, right? She's not like the others – she's different.'

Maksym hesitated, then nodded slowly. 'Maybe. But she's unpredictable. And we're in no shape to take any more risks right now.'

They sat in silence, the forest around them quiet. Dimitri knew that Sova was more than just a machine, and the thought of leaving her behind gnawed at his mind. But Maksym was right – getting Katya was a long shot, and they were running on fumes.

The silence in the forest stretched on, broken only by the occasional rustle of leaves breaking. Dimitri could see the gears turning in Maksym's head, weighing the options. Finally, Maksym stood up, pacing a little before turning back to Dimitri.

'There might be one way to make Katya work for us,' Maksym said, his voice low but charged with a new sense of purpose. 'If we can insert new code into her neural network, we could reprogram her, override whatever controls the Rusviets have in place.'

Dimitri's eyes widened. 'You can do that?'

Maksym nodded. 'It's possible, but we'd need help. I don't have the code myself, but I can try to get it from Lviv.'

Dimitri's pulse quickened. 'Lviv? Can you get a signal out from here?'

'It's risky,' Maksym replied, scanning the dense forest again, 'but I can try a direct comms link. If we're lucky, someone in Lviv can transmit the code. But we need to move. We're far from the canal, and we don't have much time before Rusviet patrols catch on.'

Dimitri felt a flicker of hope. 'So we go back to the canal, reprogram Katya, and use her to get Sova out?'

Maksym nodded, though his face was grim. 'That's the idea. But it's not a sure thing. Getting the code, reaching Katya, and actually reprogramming her – there's a lot that could go wrong. And if we fail, we'll be exposed.'

Dimitri took a deep breath, feeling the weight of the plan. 'It's worth a shot, though,' he said, meeting Maksym's gaze. 'We can't leave Sova behind.'

Maksym nodded again, then crouched down, pulling a small comms device from his pack. 'Let's see if we can reach Lviv,' he muttered, fiddling with the device. The faint hum of static filled the air as he tried to establish a connection.

The comms crackled. Then, a voice broke through the static, distorted but recognizable.

'This is Lviv Command, we read you. Code name and situation?'

Maksym wasted no time. 'Falcon Bravo Two Zero, we need reprogramming code for a T90 UX war machine. Can you send it?'

Dimitri held his breath.

'Stand by, we'll see what we can do. Transmitting the code may take time.'

Maksym nodded, glancing at Dimitri. 'I'll be making my way back to the canal,' he said into the comms. 'Send the code as soon as it's ready.'

Maksym paced for a moment, weighing the options. He turned to Dimitri, his expression serious. 'Listen, kid. I've been trained for deep undercover ops like this. Getting to the canal won't be easy, and taking you with me … it'll slow us down. You'd be a liability if we ran into trouble.'

Dimitri frowned, the weight of Maksym's words sinking in. 'But—'

'No buts,' Maksym interrupted, his tone firm. 'I need you to stay out of sight. If you're spotted, we'll both be in danger.'

Maksym scanned the surrounding trees, his eyes landing on a tall one with a thick, dense canopy. He pointed towards it. 'See that tree? It'll offer good cover. Ground scouts won't notice you, and the air drones won't be able to scan through the leaves. I need you to climb up there and stay quiet. I'll be back as soon as I can.'

Dimitri swallowed hard, glancing at the tree. It was tall, but he knew Maksym was right – he'd only slow him down. 'All right,' he said, reluctantly agreeing. 'I'll wait.'

Maksym placed a hand on Dimitri's shoulder, a rare show of camaraderie. 'You've been brave, kid. Just keep that up a little longer. I'll get the code and come back for you. We'll get Sova out.'

Dimitri nodded, feeling a knot of anxiety in his chest. He watched as Maksym gathered his gear, preparing to leave.

'Stay sharp,' Maksym added, before turning and slipping into the forest, moving with practiced stealth.

Dimitri took a deep breath and approached the tree. Heart pounding, he ascended into the thick foliage using careful movements. When he reached a sturdy branch hidden by the dense canopy, he settled in, placing his pack behind him, and tried to calm his racing thoughts.

As the forest fell into a quiet stillness, Dimitri scanned the horizon, waiting, hoping, and trusting that Maksym would come back.

Chapter 8 – Katya

Maksym moved swiftly and silently through the dense forest, keeping parallel to the train tracks. The distant groan of metal and wreckage settling into the ravine was faint now, barely carried by the wind. His senses remained sharp, years of training guiding him as he navigated the underbrush. The mission was all that mattered – reaching the canal and getting to Katya.

The trees thinned ahead, revealing a brief open stretch where the train tracks curved. Maksym slowed as he reached the treeline, scanning for signs of movement. The faint hum of drones was distant, but he knew they weren't the only threat. Scouts – especially the Velociraptors – were known to patrol these areas.

He crouched low and dashed across the exposed stretch, his steps quick and soundless. As he neared the next line of trees, a shadow shifted ahead. Maksym froze, attuning his senses to the subtle, unmistakable sound. Just beyond the treeline, a Velociraptor scout prowled, its dull grey frame blending into the forest shadows.

Maksym held his breath, flattening himself against the ground. His hand hovered near his weapon, a Mk18 CQBR short-barrelled assault rifle – but he knew that engaging the scout would be suicide. Instead, he watched, waiting. The Velociraptor paused, its sensors sweeping the area, searching for signs of life. After a few moments, the scout turned away, stalking deeper into the trees.

Maksym exhaled, rising to his feet. His pulse raced, but there was no time to waste. He pressed on, crossing the final stretch of forest until he heard the faint sound of water lapping against the banks of the canal.

Reaching the bank, Maksym scanned the murky water. There, submerged beneath layers of mud and silt, was Katya. The old war machine lay still, her optics dark and seemingly lifeless. He crouched by the water, peering at the faint outline of her massive frame.

'Still here,' he muttered under his breath.

Now came the hard part. He had to retrieve the reprogramming code from Lviv and find a way to bring Katya back online.

The forest around Dimitri smelled of pine needles and damp soil. The quiet was unnerving, broken only by the occasional rustle of dry leaves disturbed by an unseen animal. Nestled high in the dense canopy, as Maksym had instructed, his mind raced, replaying everything that had happened. Gradually, his breathing slowed, and he began to settle into his hiding spot, the leaves and branches giving him a sense of security.

For a moment, it felt almost peaceful – until a faint whirring sound broke the stillness.

A jolt of anxiety shot through Dimitri as he spotted a small, round shape darting through the trees, weaving under the canopy. The sound grew closer, and he peered through the branches, fear creeping up his temples. There, flitting among the trunks, was a ball shaped object about the size of his fist – he recognised it from a movie he'd once seen as a Rusviet Mini Scout.

It glided silently through the air. These scouts were notorious for their ability to search wide areas at low altitude, and they were designed for one purpose: finding humans. Though unarmed, the scout's presence meant danger. It scanned the trees nearby, likely drawn by the wreckage of the train.

Dimitri pressed his back against the thick trunk, trying to steady his breath. The Mini Scout hovered near a tree just a few meters away, its single red eye sweeping back and forth. Paralysis gripped him. If the scout detected him, it would call in reinforcements.

Slowly, with painstaking care, Dimitri reached into his pack. His fingers closed around the cold metal of the pistol, owned once by Sova's previous pilot. Every muscle in his body tensed as he pulled it free, keeping his movements deliberate, quiet.

The scout's whirring grew louder. It was moving closer.

Dimitri's heart pounded in his ears as the small drone hovered just below his position. He held his breath, watching it from above, willing it to move on. As he shifted ever so slightly, the noise of his movement caught the scout's attention.

The drone froze, then whirred loudly, popping up to Dimitri's eye level, its sensor locking onto him. Panic surged through Dimitri, but instinct kicked in. Without thinking, he raised his pistol, aiming directly at the scout's glowing red eye.

He pulled the trigger.

The shot rang out, shattering the silence. The Mini Scout sparked, its red eye flickering before it fell from the air, trailing smoke as it crashed into the forest floor below. Dimitri sat frozen, his heart racing, adrenaline coursing through his veins as he watched the scout's small frame twitch and smoulder in the dirt.

The eery quiet returned to the forest.

Maksym crouched at the edge of the canal, the afternoon sun casting long shadows across the water. The daylight made everything more exposed, heightening his urgency to move quickly. His comms crackled to life, and the transmission began. He watched the device carefully, breathing deeply as the reprogramming code downloaded.

When the transmission finished, Maksym didn't hesitate. He secured his gear, removed his jacket, and waded into the canal's murky water. The cold water shocked him, but he pushed forward, swimming towards Katya's submerged form.

The sunlight barely penetrated the depths, casting a greenish hue over the water as Maksym reached the submerged machine. Katya lay still beneath the surface of the canal, her frame partially sunk into the mud beneath. He located the access port on her side, pulling out the probe and inserting it into her neural interface.

Bubbles rose as her systems stirred to life. The water rippled, and a faint hum vibrated through her chassis. Maksym glimpsed the flickering of Katya's red optics under the surface, glowing more brightly as her programming adjusted.

Her voice crackled through his earpiece, slightly raspy yet unmistakably aware: 'Reprogramming complete. Alliance changed. Maksym Melnyk designated as Pilot.'

Maksym allowed himself a brief nod of relief. It had worked.

Katya shifted in the mud, her massive form beginning to power up. 'Memories retained. Mission parameters updated,' she added, her fatigued tone steady but sharper now, understanding her new purpose.

Maksym tapped his earpiece, adjusting to her frequency. 'Get your cockpit above the water line but stay low. We're too exposed in daylight. We'll use your arms to swim through the canal. No surfacing until I say so.'

Katya responded without hesitation. 'Acknowledged.'

Maksym approached her now partly emerged form, reaching for the panel that concealed the cockpit entrance. With a sharp hiss, the hatch slid open, releasing a burst of compressed air as the seals disengaged. Water beaded on the metal surface, and steam rose from the subtle warmth inside the machine. Maksym hesitated, then pulled himself up and into the cockpit, the metal cold and slick beneath his hands.

As he settled into the pilot's seat, the interior lights flickered to life, casting a dim glow over the controls. The hatch hissed shut behind him, sealing with a satisfying click. Katya's cockpit dropped back beneath the water's surface, facing forward in a swimming position. Water dripped from Maksym's clothes and pooled at his feet as he secured himself in the harness.

He took a deep breath and scanned the surrounding forest through Katya's external sensors, the display screens flickering to show the treeline and the shimmering surface of the canal. All clear – for now. Maksym tapped the console, his fingers flying over the controls.

'Katya,' he murmured, 'let's move.'

Katya's giant frame shifted beneath the water with silent grace, her bulk barely disturbing the murky surface as they glided forward, hidden from view. Maksym watched the flow of water above and around the cockpit.

The sun hung high, making every ripple in the canal more visible. Maksym's pulse quickened as he urged Katya forward, their progress controlled and deliberate. They approached the treeline, the dense foliage ahead promising safety.

'Surface now, but keep low,' Maksym instructed.

Katya rose slowly, moving with remarkable silence for a machine of her size. Water cascaded off her metal plating as she slipped under the cover of the trees. Maksym surveyed the area, the sunlight filtering through the canopy to cast shadows on the forest floor. He watched for any sign of drones or scouts before giving the final command.

Once satisfied they were in the clear, he spoke through his comms piece. 'We're in the trees now Move low but increase speed – we need to reach Dimitri quickly.'

Katya responded by moving seamlessly into the forest, disappearing under the cover of the dense foliage, the glaring daylight above unable to betray their path.

Hours had passed since Maksym left, and Dimitri's muscles ached from crouching among the jagged rocks that formed his new hiding place. He shifted, wincing as his knee scraped against the rough stone, trying to stretch his legs without making a sound. On one side, a cluster of bushes provided cover, their dense branches weaving together like a natural shield. The rocks beneath him were cold and unyielding, their chill seeping through his thin clothing. The forest around him was eerily still; each creak of the foliage amplified the silence. Just as he began to ease into the discomfort, a sound pierced the quiet – a faint rustling, too deliberate to be the wind. A low clank echoed through the trees, followed by the unmistakable hum of something large approaching. Dimitri's heart skipped a beat. He froze, straining his ears. The sound grew louder – closer – until he could make out the distinct footfalls of multiple machines.

Velociraptors. Panic seized him. They must have picked up the Mini Scout's last transmission.

Dimitri shifted his weight carefully, looking for a direction to run. If they found him … his fingers brushed the pistol at his side. There would be no hiding after that.

They weren't far now. Dimitri's body tensed. The bush, rocks and even shadows offered some protection, but it wouldn't last if they tracked him.

He risked a glance over his shoulder just as two Velociraptors arrived at the base of the tree where he had previously hidden. Their sleek, metallic frames gleamed in the dim light. One of them craned its neck upward, inspecting the tree. The other paced in a slow circle, its sensors sweeping the ground.

Dimitri swallowed hard, his pulse racing. He couldn't wait for Maksym to help him.

Without wasting another second, he crept away from the danger, every muscle taut as he distanced himself. Every breath he took felt shallow, his ears trained for the slightest hint of pursuit. The forest grew denser around him, but he knew it wouldn't be enough to lose them.

Ahead, the ground sloped downward, and the sound of rushing water reached his ears. Dimitri quickened his pace, heart pounding with hope. A fast-moving stream cut through the forest, surrounded by thick bushes and jagged rocks. He paused at the edge, glancing back. The Velociraptors would be on him soon.

A memory surfaced: Sova, hiding in the cold waters of the river to mask her heat signature. If it worked for her …

With no time to hesitate, Dimitri climbed into the freezing stream, the water immediately pulling at him. He

120

gritted his teeth against the cold and lay on his back, submerging his body as much as possible, his face just below the surface. The stream's current was strong, tugging at his clothes, but he anchored his boots against a large rock, keeping himself in place.

His lungs screamed and he held his breath, trying to fix his eyes on the forest line through the rushing water. Moments later, the Velociraptors appeared. Their tall, sleek frames moved with eerie precision, sensors scanning the area. They paused near the water's edge, tilting their heads as if confused.

Dimitri's chest burned. He fought the desperate urge to gasp for air as the Velociraptors stalked up and down the stream, their sensors clearly struggling to locate his heat signature. *Come on ... turn back ... please ...*

Seconds felt like minutes. Just as his vision began to blur from lack of air, the Velociraptors heads snapped in another direction. They turned, taloned feet carrying them away, deeper into the forest.

Dimitri started to see stars before he broke the surface, gasping for air. His lungs felt like they were on fire, and his body shivered from the cold. He dragged himself out of the stream and collapsed onto the bank, his chest heaving.

For a few moments, he lay there, too exhausted to move, letting the adrenaline slowly ebb from his system. But the cold was biting, relentless, and the freezing water had soaked through his clothes and into his bag. His shivering became uncontrollable, his fingers stiff and clumsy as he tried to push himself up.

You must keep moving, he thought, forcing himself to stand. His legs trembled beneath him, weak from both fear and exposure. He cast a glance around, making sure the Velociraptors were truly gone. The forest was quiet again, the only sound the distant rush of the stream.

Dimitri staggered a few steps, his soaked boots squelching in the mud as he moved away from the stream and the tree where he had initially hidden. His muscles ached from the cold, and his hands shook as he tried to grip the straps of his pack. *It's not safe here,* he thought. *I need to hide.*

His teeth chattered, the cold seeping deep into his bones. He spotted a dense bush nearby, its thick branches offering a semblance of cover. Dimitri half-crawled, half-stumbled towards it and dropped to his knees, pulling at the branches with trembling hands. He piled them over himself, curling into a ball beneath the canopy of leaves.

As minutes went on, the cold deepened its hold on him. His shivering worsened, his body trying to generate heat, but the wet clothes clinging to his skin only made it worse. His fingers were numb, his mind sluggish. *I have to get warm ... but how?*

Another hour or so passed in a blur of cold and fatigue. Dimitri's teeth chattered violently, his limbs stiff and uncooperative. Hypothermia was setting in. He wouldn't last much longer like this.

The Velociraptors were nowhere to be seen, but if he stayed like this, hidden and freezing, he'd die long before they came back.

I need a fire.

It was a risk – starting a fire might draw attention – but the cold was unbearable. He had no other choice. Slowly, painfully, Dimitri pulled himself from the bush. His soaked clothes weighed him down as he staggered into the nearby underbrush, gathering twigs, dry leaves, and anything he could use as fuel. His hands shook so badly that he nearly dropped half of it as he worked.

Once he had enough, Dimitri crouched low, trying to shield himself from the cold wind threading through the trees. He pulled the fire starter from his sodden bag. It was wet like everything else, but he struck it again and again, hoping the spark would catch. Each failed attempt sent a wave of frustration and desperation through him.

Finally, a spark caught on a small pile of dry brush. He fanned it gently, his breath misting in the cool air, and watched as the tiny flames grew, licking at the twigs and leaves. Relief washed over him as the fire crackled to life.

Dimitri huddled over the small fire; his body drawn as close to it as possible. The warmth began to seep into his chilled skin, but his clothes were still wet, and the fire wasn't enough to dry them. A cool breeze blew through the woods, cutting through the meagre warmth like a knife. He shivered, pulling his arms tightly around himself as he tried to absorb as much heat as possible.

The fire was pitiful, barely enough to ward off the lingering chill, but it was better than nothing. Slowly, the heat returned to his fingers and face, though the rest of him remained drenched and cold. His breath came in shallow, shivering gasps, but at least he was no longer shaking uncontrollably.

The crackle of the flames comforted him, and for the first time since the Velociraptors arrived, Dimitri allowed himself a moment to breathe. He knew he couldn't stay here for long. Once he warmed up, he'd have to move again to keep ahead of the machines. And the fire itself was a risk.

With the cold biting less sharply, he stamped out the small flames, scattering the remaining embers into the dirt.

It was time to go back – to the ravine where Sova lay motionless beneath the wreckage. *Maybe Maksym will find me there,* he thought, trying to suppress the creeping dread in his chest. *If he's still alive.*

Dimitri stepped carefully through the forest, the underbrush crunching beneath his boots. The sun had passed its highest point, and the afternoon light cast long shadows across the trees, but with each step, the weight of uncertainty gnawed at him. *How long will I have to wait at the ravine?* he wondered, hoping that Maksym would show up sooner rather than later.

The forest thinned as Dimitri approached the edge of the ravine. The ground sloped downward into jagged rocks, leading to the shattered remains of the train far below. His breath caught as he looked out over the scene. Even though he'd seen it before, the devastation was overwhelming. The wreckage was scattered across the ravine, half-buried in earth and twisted metal.

At the heart of it lay Sova.

The monstrous T90 had crashed down on top of her, half-burying her in debris. Her gleaming metal surface was scratched and scarred from the battle. The once-mighty war machine now lay lifeless, motionless, trapped under the weight of her enemy.

Dimitri's heart sank. She saved me. But now she was … broken. Helpless. He felt an overwhelming sense of guilt, even though there was nothing he could've done to prevent what had happened.

He sat at the edge of the ravine, legs dangling over the precipice. The sun's light was growing softer, and the long shadows stretched further into the distance. How long would he wait here? Would Maksym come for him? Would anyone?

The wind shifted, rustling the leaves around him. Dimitri tensed, the creeping feeling of being watched crawling up his spine. He turned his head, scanning the forest. Nothing. Just trees and shadows.

He turned back towards the wreckage below. Time seemed to stretch in the silence, the weight of the moment pressing down on him. The ravine felt so vast, so empty.

Then – a sound. A soft, unmistakable click.

Dimitri's blood turned to ice. That sound … he had heard it before.

Slowly, dread settling in his stomach, he turned around.

A few hundred feet away, looming in the shadows of the trees, stood two Velociraptors. Their predatory figures blended almost perfectly with the dappled light. Their glowing eyes locked on him, weapons raised and aimed with cold precision.

Dimitri's froze.

The lead Velociraptor took a single step forward, its joints hissing as it moved. The muzzle of its weapon didn't waver, trained squarely on Dimitri's chest.

There was nowhere to run. Nowhere to hide. He was pinned against the edge of the ravine, the drop behind him far too steep to descend without risking a deadly fall.

His heart raced as he realized his only option: he'd have to face them. But how?

For a long moment, neither of the machines moved. Then, the one in front tilted its head slightly, its glowing eyes narrowing as though sizing him up. A synthetic voice crackled to life – harsh, grating, and emotionless.

'You. Will. Follow.'

The voice rasped against Dimitri's ears, as though the Velociraptor was speaking through layers of distortion. The robotic inflection left no room for negotiation. It was a command, not a request.

Dimitri's throat tightened. He blinked, struggling to process what he had just heard. Follow? He stared at the machine, wondering why they hadn't simply captured him outright – or worse.

The second Velociraptor, stationed behind the first, took a single step forward, its weapon unwavering. Dimitri's mind raced, searching for an escape, but there was none.

The lead Velociraptor's eyes flared as it spoke again, its voice sharper, more insistent.

'Follow. Or be eliminated.'

Dimitri took a slow step forward, the cold wind stinging through his soaked clothes. His legs felt heavy as he began to walk towards the machines, his mind a blur of questions and fear.

As they ventured deeper back into the forest, something massive came into view. A quiet elation rose within him as out from the trees emerged a familiar shape, its old, battered frame unmistakable – Katya. Her worn body looked just as it had the last time he'd seen her, albeit streaked with more dried mud from the canal.

But it was the pilot that held Dimitri's attention. From his vantage point, he could just make out the familiar silhouette inside. Maksym.

Katya's optics flared to life, her voice booming as she addressed the Velociraptors. 'What are you doing with this prisoner?'

The Velociraptors paused, turning to face the war machine. One of them stepped forward, unfazed by her sudden presence. 'We are escorting a resistance fighter, as per protocol.'

Katya's optics flickered again. 'I'll take it from here,' she said, her voice commanding. 'My orders are to escort the prisoner myself. You are no longer needed.'

The Velociraptors hesitated, unsure. One of them, more cautious than the other, took a step back. 'Orders? From where?' it asked, its tone edged with suspicion. A soft click emanated from its head as an internal transmitter activated, preparing to relay the query to central command.

Maksym's voice cut through the tension from the cockpit. 'Dimitri, duck!'

Dimitri dropped to the ground just as the air erupted with gunfire. Katya's cannons roared to life, her Autocannons unleashing a hail of high explosive rounds at the Velociraptors. The machines scrambled to respond, but it was too late – Maksym had the upper hand.

The Velociraptors returned fire, but they were no match for Katya's size and firepower. The first unit was torn apart instantly, collapsing in a heap of sparks. The remaining Velociraptor attempted to run, but Maksym was relentless. He controlled Katya with precision, taking aim and firing again. The Velociraptor fell, body crashing to the ground, shattered and smoking.

Dimitri lay on the ground, his heart pounding in his chest. Slowly, he looked up to see Katya towering over him, her optics still glowing. Maksym's voice crackled over the comms.

'Dimitri, you okay?'

Dimitri nodded, his breath shaky as he stood up. 'Yeah,' he muttered, glancing at the smoking wreckage of the Velociraptors. 'Thanks to you.'

Chapter 9 – Rescue

Nightfall was fast approaching, casting long shadows through the trees as the trio made their way towards the ravine. Maksym and Dimitri shared Katya's dimly lit cockpit, its utilitarian design a stark contrast to Sova's more advanced interior. The space felt cramped, with its aged controls and worn surfaces bearing the marks of countless missions. Movement was limited – the seating prioritised efficiency over comfort – but the journey was too dangerous to attempt on foot. The low hum of Katya's systems filled the otherwise silent, darkening forest.

'There's an old track nearby,' Maksym muttered, scanning the terrain through Katya's external sensors. 'It should take us down to the ravine floor. From there, we can check the wreckage.'

Dimitri nodded, his body tense from both the cramped quarters and the looming uncertainty. His stomach felt tight, probably from worry. The closer they got to the ravine, the heavier the weight of the task seemed to grow. He pulled Maksym's oversized jersey tighter around himself, which smelled faintly of oil and earth.

Cramped though they were, the warmth of the cockpit and the jersey offered some relief from the lingering dampness that still clung to Dimitri's clothes. His thoughts kept drifting to the task ahead – finding Sova, buried beneath the wreckage – but for now, he held onto the warmth as best as he could.

The track wound downward, cutting through the steep cliffs until the floor of the ravine came into view. The remains of the train were scattered across the rocky terrain, a twisted mess of metal and debris. One of the carriages had carried ammunition – evident by the massive crater it had left behind.

As they reached the bottom, Maksym's eyes darted around, scanning for any signs of drones. But the air was still, and no hum of machines could be heard. 'They think it's all destroyed,' Maksym said, more to himself than to Dimitri.

Katya moved forward, her sensors active as they neared the wreckage. 'There,' Dimitri whispered, pointing. Beneath the ruins of the final carriage, he could make out Sova's battered form buried under the T90 she had been battling.

They approached cautiously. Sova's body lay partially hidden by the debris, her chest plate dented, her optics dark. Maksym leaned forward, frowning.

Katya's voice broke the silence, calm and analytical. 'Engaging scan.' Her sensors flickered to life, bathing the wreckage in a soft glow as she analysed Sova's systems. Data streamed across the cockpit's display as Katya's scanners searched for a way to power Sova back on.

At first, nothing happened. Then, Katya spoke again. 'Power core is intact but inaccessible. Secondary systems offline. There is a bypass option – if I can lift the T90 off her, we may be able to engage an auxiliary reboot.'

Katya's mechanical limbs groaned as she strained to lift the wrecked T90. Metal scraped against metal, the debris shifting inch by inch as her servos powered through the weight. Maksym and Dimitri, having climbed from the cockpit, stood nearby, ready to jump in as the T90 was slowly lifted. With a final push, Katya managed to clear the last of the wreckage, shoving the ruined machine aside.

Sova's body, though battered and dust-covered, was now free. Dimitri rushed forward, his eyes filled with concern. 'Is she ...?'

Katya's optics flickered. 'Attempting ignition sequence.' A hidden panel in her arm slid open to reveal a series of engineering tools. With delicate precision, she connected a cable to a port beneath Sova's right arm, sending a surge of power through her system. A hum began to resonate through Sova's frame, and the lights in her optics flickered back to life – dim at first, then brighter.

Sova's voice crackled, weak but unmistakable. 'Last memory ... the fall ... I engaged the enemy T90, but the force of the crash ... I couldn't hold on.' Her words were fragmented, as if her systems were still rebooting. 'Impact ... then darkness.'

Dimitri knelt beside her large dusty cockpit, his hand stroking the glass, relief washing over him. 'You're back,' he whispered, though Sova's condition was far from stable. Katya, ever the engineer, scanned Sova's frame, quickly assessing the damage.

'Multiple fractures in the hull. Power core is functional but secondary systems are down. Repairs are possible but limited.' Katya extended a tool from her arm, a mechanical torch flaring to life. With delicate movements, she began welding the damaged sections of Sova's frame, patching up the worst of the cracks. 'I can stabilise her, but she won't be fully operational without a proper repair facility.'

Maksym, who had been scouting the area, returned just as Katya finished her repairs. His eyes lit up with determination. 'I found an old track,' he said, pointing towards the western side of the ravine towards Lviv. 'It's steep though.'

Dimitri glanced at Sova's immobile form. 'But how ...?'

Katya moved to the wreckage of the train, scanning the debris. 'We'll need to fashion a sled,' she said, her voice matter of fact. Her arms worked quickly, cutting through the twisted metal of the carriages with her built-in tools. Piece by piece, she fashioned a massive sled, welding together long metal beams to create a sturdy platform capable of supporting Sova's weight.

Once finished, Katya carefully dragged Sova onto the sled. It groaned under the weight but held firm. Amongst the wreckage, Maksym had discovered thick steel cables, once used to secure freight. Katya, with deft precision, had detached them from the debris and fashioned a harness.

Maksym tested the tension of the steel cables now wrapped against Sova and the sled, securing it to Katya's frame. 'Think you can pull this thing up the track?' he asked, his voice tinged with uncertainty.

Katya's optics dimmed momentarily, her voice even. 'With my strength, yes. But it will be slow.'

Nightfall had settled in, casting the entire ravine into near-total darkness. Katya's optics and low spotlight provided the only light, along with a shimmer of the moon filtering behind darkened clouds. Shadows stretched across the path as the trio began their ascent.

With a deep vibration, Katya took hold of the steel cables, her towering frame nearly as tall as a two-story building, her powerful limbs braced against the ground, digging into the earth for traction. The path was steep, the incline daunting, but she began to pull. Inch by inch, the massive sled scraped against dirt and small rocks, Sova's heavy frame resting atop it as they began the long, arduous climb up the ravine.

Dimitri and Maksym walked behind, Katya trudging up front in complete darkness to keep them nearly invisible as they ascended. The trio's footsteps were careful and deliberate, eyes constantly scanning the blackened horizon for any signs of trouble. The stillness of the night was unnerving, broken only by the creaking sled on the stone-strewn path and Katya's heavy footfalls.

After several hours, the group finally crested the top of the ravine. The open terrain opened into a dense forest, the leafy canopy above providing a much-needed cover from any prying eyes in the sky. Maksym surveyed the area, assessing the terrain and the stillness of the forest. The soft rustling of leaves in the breeze mixed with an unmistakable woodsy scent create a sense of eerie calm.

Maksym glanced at Dimitri and saw the exhaustion written all over his young face: dark circles under his eyes, the slight wobble in his step. Dimitri was tough, but the day's efforts had taken their toll. Maksym sighed, his instincts telling him it was time to rest.

'We'll camp here inside the treeline,' Maksym said, his voice gentle but firm. 'No point pushing any further tonight.'

Dimitri blinked up at him, a mixture of relief and fatigue crossing his features. 'Here? In the forest?'

Maksym nodded. 'We're hidden under the canopy. It's as safe a spot as any.'

Katya finally came to a halt, the sled resting quietly now that the hard part was over. Dimitri sank to the ground, his legs grateful for the break. Maksym found a small clearing where the trees were tightly packed, creating a natural shelter from the elements. He began gathering fallen branches and dried leaves to form a makeshift fire pit.

Within minutes, the warm crackle of a small fire came to life, its light flickering across the group. The heat was a welcome change from the chill that had settled in as night began to fall. Dimitri stretched out his legs, leaning against a tree, his eyes drawn to the flickering flames as he let out a long, weary breath.

From his pack, Maksym produced a handful of dried meat and a small pouch of berries he'd scavenged earlier. He passed them to Dimitri, who took them gratefully, though his movements were sluggish.

'Eat,' Maksym instructed. 'You'll feel better.'

Dimitri nodded, chewing slowly on the tough meat, its salty taste grounding him in the moment. The berries, sweet and slightly tart, burst with flavour as he ate, providing a much-needed energy boost. Beside him, Katya stood watch, her optics scanning the perimeter, ever vigilant.

Maksym sat down beside Dimitri, tearing into his own share of the meal, his eyes glancing at the boy. 'You did well today,' he said after a moment, his voice softer than usual. 'Not many could keep up with this kind of pace.'

Dimitri didn't answer, his gaze still fixed on the fire. He felt the warmth of Maksym's words but didn't know how to respond. His body ached, and his mind was already slipping towards the comfort of sleep.

As the night deepened, the fire became the only light in the forest, casting long shadows around them. The soft crackle of burning wood filled the silence, and for the first time that day, Dimitri felt the weight of the journey lift from his shoulders, even if he knew the feeling wouldn't last.

Maksym glanced up at Katya, who stood motionless, barely shifting as the cool breeze rustled through the leaves around her. She was a reassuring presence, silent and strong, guarding them while they rested.

'We'll head out at first light,' Maksym said quietly. He threw another small branch onto the fire, watching the sparks dance into the night. 'But for now, we sleep.'

Dimitri, already lying down, let his eyes close as exhaustion claimed him. The warmth of the fire wrapped around him like a blanket, and the sounds of the forest blended into a soothing lullaby.

As he drifted off, he heard Maksym's voice, soft and reassuring: 'Rest now, kid. We've made it this far. Tomorrow's another day.'

The forest stood silent around them, the canopy of trees a protective shield from the chaos beyond. For now, they were safe. And that was enough.

Chapter 10 – Frontline

The fire had long since died down, leaving only the faint glow of embers casting dim shadows around the campsite. The air was crisp and cool, the stillness of the forest unbroken except for the soft rustle of leaves in the breeze. Maksym stirred first, his soldier instincts bringing him to full alertness long before dawn.

He rose quietly, glancing around the camp. Dimitri was still curled up by the remains of the fire, his breathing slow and steady. Katya, standing tall and silent as ever, appeared to be in Deep Sleep mode, her optics dim and unmoving. Sova's battered frame lay unmoving on the makeshift sled.

Maksym crouched beside Dimitri, giving him a gentle shake. 'Time to get up, kid,' he said softly. 'We've got a long trek ahead of us.'

Dimitri groaned, blinking awake and rubbing his eyes, the grogginess of sleep clinging to him. 'Already?' he mumbled, glancing up at the still-dark sky.

'Yup. The sooner we move, the better,' Maksym replied, offering a hand to help him sit up. 'Eat something if you're hungry. We're heading to Lviv today.'

Dimitri nodded, still half-asleep, and reached for the last of the dried berries from the night before. He ate quietly, watching Maksym move with military efficiency, packing their meagre supplies and checking the area for signs of activity.

Maksym's eyes flicked towards Katya. 'Time to wake her up.'

He walked over to the towering war machine and touched her giant arm, prompting a low, mechanical whir as Katya slowly came back online.

'Good morning, Maksym,' Katya's voice rumbled through the quiet forest. 'It seems I am still operational, despite my advanced age.'

Maksym smiled, leaning against a tree as he watched her finish booting up. 'You're not that old, Katya. I've seen worse.'

Katya's optics flickered in what might have been the robotic equivalent of an eye roll. 'Old enough to remember when they built these trees, perhaps.'

Dimitri, now more awake and munching on the last of his berries, stifled a laugh. 'She's got you there.'

Maksym shook his head, a grin tugging at the corners of his mouth. 'You sure you're up for this trip, old girl? I wouldn't want you to throw a gear out on the way to Lviv.'

'I assure you, Maksym, I am more than capable of completing this journey. Though, if anyone should be concerned about their age, it may be you. How are your knees holding up?'

Dimitri snickered at that, and Maksym shot Katya a mock glare. 'My knees are fine. Just make sure you don't fall behind, or I'll have to leave you in the dust.'

Katya's voice took on a playfully serious tone. 'I would like to see you try, Commander.'

Shaking his head, Maksym finished packing up the last of their gear, the light banter between them helping to ease the tension that had been building since the night before. Dimitri stretched his legs, feeling a little more awake, and rose to his feet.

'All right,' Maksym said. 'We head out now. We stick to the trees as much as possible and keep a low profile until we reach Lviv.'

Dimitri slung his small pack over his shoulder and nodded. 'What about Sova? Can she move?'

Katya turned her optics towards Sova, who still lay motionless on the sled. 'She will be operational once we arrive in Lviv. I just need more parts and resources. Until then, she remains immobile and will remain in Deep Sleep mode.'

Maksym nodded. 'Good. Let's get moving then. Katya, we're going to ride with you for now.'

Katya, towering above them, lowered herself to the ground, servos whirring softly.

Katya's cockpit hatch hissed open, revealing the interior. Dimitri climbed in first, feeling the rugged and well-worn chair on his hand, old cables coiled around the seats, and the machinery humming gently underfoot. Dimitri felt a strange sense of comfort here, the cockpit's worn-in feel giving it character. Maksym joined him, squeezing in beside with a *humpf.*

Once they were settled in, the hatch closed, and Katya's deep voice filled the cockpit. 'Are you comfortable?'

'More or less,' Maksym said, smirking slightly. 'It's a tight fit, but I think we'll manage.'

Dimitri chuckled, trying to find a comfortable position in the cramped space.

With them secured inside, Katya powered up, her systems humming to life around them. She approached the sled, where Sova still lay, and reached down to pick up the steel cables of the harness. She slipped the straps over her shoulders, the sled groaning as the weight shifted.

The cockpit vibrated as Katya adjusted her stance, ready to pull. Dimitri could feel the subtle tension in the controls as she prepared for the haul.

'Let's get Sova to Lviv,' Maksym said, his tone more serious now.

Katya didn't respond verbally, but the hum of her systems deepened as she leaned forward, her powerful servos straining as she began to drag Sova once again. The sled creaked under the immense weight, but this ground was softer than the incline the night before, and

Katya's strength didn't falter. Foot by foot, she moved forward, pulling Sova across the forest floor.

Inside the cockpit, Dimitri watched the trees pass by, his thoughts drifting back to the skirmish at the river a couple of days earlier. He had tried – and failed – to shoot down a Viper with Sova's cannon, missing every shot before Maksym saved them both with a well-timed missile. The memory still gnawed at him.

Maksym gave the boy a sidelong glance and grinned. 'You've got the potential, kid, but I saw you fumbling with Sova's cannon back at the river. How about we do something about that?'

Dimitri looked up, surprised. 'You mean, now?'

'Why not?' Maksym shrugged. 'No better time. You're going to need that skill, and I'd rather you learn here than in the middle of a firefight again.' He leaned forward slightly and addressed Katya. 'Katya, bring up the cannon controls, just like in Sova's cockpit.'

Katya's optics flickered, and moments later, the familiar cannon controls materialized in front of Dimitri, projected as a holographic interface. The layout was identical to Sova's, complete with the targeting system that Dimitri had struggled with at the river.

The memory of his missed shots played in Dimitri's mind. But this was different – there was no real Viper, no immediate danger. Maybe this time, he could actually hit the target.

'All right, kid,' Maksym said, settling in. 'We're going to run a sim. Picture a Viper drone coming straight at you. Your job is to bring it down before it gets too close. Let's see how you handle it.'

Katya's calm voice filled the cockpit. 'Simulated target: Sui-77 Viper Class Attack Drone approaching. Prepare to engage.'

On the display, a virtual Viper appeared, rapidly closing in. Its sleek frame was all too familiar, its speed unnerving. Dimitri's pulse quickened as he gripped the controls.

'Remember what happened at the river?' Maksym asked, his voice steady. 'This time, you get to learn without the pressure.'

Dimitri exhaled, trying to stay calm. He lined up the sights, tracking the Viper as it approached. But just like before, panic set in. The drone moved too fast, and he fired too soon. The shot whizzed wide, completely missing the target.

The Viper simulated a strafing attack, darting past them in a blur.

Dimitri slumped in his seat, frustrated. 'I missed again.'

Maksym chuckled, though his tone was encouraging. 'You're rushing it. You're trying to hit where the Viper is, not where it's going to be. The trick is to lead the shot. Watch how it moves, and aim for where it will be, not where it is.'

Dimitri frowned, still gripping the controls. He wanted to get this right. 'But it's so fast. How do I even know where it's going?'

'Trust your instincts,' Maksym said, leaning back slightly. 'You can't rely just on the targeting system. You've seen these things in action before. Focus on the movement. Predict the trajectory.'

Dimitri nodded, taking a deep breath. He needed to calm down, to stop chasing the target and anticipate it instead.

'Katya, reset the sim,' Maksym instructed.

'Simulated target re-engaged: Sui-77 Drone approaching,' Katya responded.

The Viper appeared again, racing towards them. This time, Dimitri didn't rush. He watched carefully, noticing the way the drone zigzagged in its approach. He waited, his finger hovering over the trigger, his eyes locked on the target.

Maksym's advice echoed in his mind: lead the shot.

As the Viper banked left, Dimitri moved the cannon slightly ahead of its trajectory and squeezed the trigger. The cannon fired, and this time the shot clipped the Viper's wing. It wasn't a direct hit, but the damage was enough to send the drone spiralling. It crashed into the virtual ground, debris scattering across the display.

Dimitri let out a breath he didn't realize he'd been holding, a wave of relief washing over him. He hadn't nailed it, but he'd brought it down.

Maksym clapped him on the shoulder, grinning. 'Not bad, kid. You winged the bastard.'

Dimitri grinned back, the frustration from earlier replaced with a growing sense of pride. 'I actually hit it.'

'And next time, you'll hit it dead-on,' Maksym said. 'Remember what you felt just now. That's how you take control in a real fight.'

Katya's voice chimed in, her tone calm but approving. 'Simulation complete. Good effort, Dimitri. Should I prepare another target?'

Dimitri shook his head, still catching his breath. 'Maybe later,' he said, not willing to gamble on his newly formed confidence. He sat back in the cockpit, feeling like he had taken a real step forward.

As the forest passed by slowly outside the cockpit, Dimitri leaned back, the adrenaline from the simulated Viper attack still coursing through his veins. He felt more confident now, but there was a lingering tension in the air. The trek to Lviv wasn't just a long one – it was dangerous.

'Katya,' Maksym said, sensing Dimitri's unease, 'bring up a map of our current location. I want to see where we are in relation to the front lines.'

Katya's optics flickered in acknowledgment, and a large holographic map materialized before them. The map displayed their position deep in the forest, with the surrounding terrain stretching out in every direction. To the north, a faint red line pulsed, marking the known front where the Rusviet forces were holding position.

'We're here,' Maksym said, pointing to their location on the map, which was still just south of the front line. 'But we're closing in on a stretch that's seen heavy fighting.'

Dimitri leaned forward, his eyes scanning the map. His stomach tightened as he saw how close they were getting to that red line. 'How close are we?'

Katya's voice answered smoothly, 'Approximately ten kilometres from the current front line. However, enemy patrols have been reported as far south as five kilometres from this point.'

Maksym rubbed his jaw, frowning at the map. 'We're heading straight for a dangerous zone,' he said, his voice low but calm. 'The Rusviets have AI patrols sweeping this whole area. If we're not careful, we'll run right into them.'

Dimitri's heart began to race again, not from excitement this time, but from the realization of how close they were to the danger zone. 'So … what do we do?'

Maksym was silent for a moment, studying the map. He traced a potential path through the forest with his finger, his brow furrowed. 'We stay hidden as much as possible. Katya will need to keep a low profile. We can't afford to have her out in the open dragging Sova. We'll use the thickest parts of the forest to shield us from drones and patrols.'

Katya's voice interjected. 'I can detect airborne surveillance within a five-kilometre radius. I will alert you to any nearby threats.'

Maksym nodded. 'Good. Keep your sensors active.'

Dimitri stared at the map, feeling the weight of the situation settle over him.

'We've got about a day before we hit the edge of that zone,' Maksym said, sitting back and folding his arms. 'We'll stop just before it gets too risky. For now, we keep moving, but with more caution.'

Dimitri nodded, his mind already racing with thoughts of what lay ahead. The safety of the forest felt thinner now, less of a barrier and more of a fragile shield.

Maksym glanced at him, his expression unreadable. 'Remember, kid – this isn't just a trek to Lviv. We're entering a battlefield. And once we're in it, there's no turning back.'

Katya's optics dimmed as she prepared to resume towing Sova. 'I will begin scanning for nearby threats immediately,' she said, her voice reassuring.

Maksym gave her a sharp nod from within the cockpit. 'Good. I'm going to go ahead and scout the best path forward from here – you follow my trail. Dimitri, use the spare comms unit in case things heat up.'

Katya lowered herself to let Maksym out. After checking his gear and slinging his MK18 across his shoulder, Maksym slipped between the trees, his movements smooth and deliberate, his footfalls barely a whisper on the forest floor.

An hour later, hidden just inside the treeline, Maksym surveyed the scene using his scope. The Ukrainians were holding their ground on this section of the battlefield, but barely. The landscape was potted with the remnants of trees, their trunks shattered by artillery fire. Rolling hills stretched in every direction, providing some cover, though much of it had been levelled in the relentless advance. There were two Rusviet T90 Volks moving steadily across the terrain, their heavy armour glinting under the dim light of flares in the sky. Ukrainian troops were pinned down, entrenched in craters and behind the remains of fallen trees, exchanging sporadic fire, and the overwhelming firepower of the T90s made the situation desperate.

Maksym's heart pounded as he assessed the enemy's positions. The Volks had yet to detect his group, but they would need precision timing to launch their attack from behind. He could see the weak points in their formation –

gaps that Katya could exploit if they moved swiftly enough. But the enemy was well-supported, and what appeared to be a Viper attack drone circling above presented another obstacle.

He tapped his earpiece. 'I've got eyes on the enemy. Two Volks are advancing on the Resistance, one Viper overhead. We have a window, but it's narrow. We strike now, or we miss the chance.'

A moment of silence followed, and then Dimitri's voice came through, steady but tense. 'Understood. We're ready.'

As Maksym made his way back to the group, Sova stirred slightly from her hiding place, a flicker of power running through her systems. Maksym's instincts kicked in – this battle was about to turn, and they would need every bit of strength they had left to pull it off.

Lying beneath the forest canopy, Sova's systems flickered back to life, damaged but functional. She processed the battlefield, and despite her condition, Sova made her decision.

Opportunity detected, Sova murmured into Dimitri's earpiece. He blinked in surprise. 'She's … she's not ready for this,' Dimitri whispered, looking towards the treeline where Sova lay.

But Sova had already made her choice. With a creaking groan, she pulled herself from the undergrowth, dented and damaged, but still determined. She limped from the shadows, her great form barely stable, one leg limping as she advanced towards the giant Volks.

'Dimitri,' Maksym hissed through his comms. 'What is she doing?'

'She's engaging,' Dimitri replied from Katya's cockpit, shock and concern mixing in his voice.

As Sova moved forward, her 20mm cannon sputtered to life, the rounds finding their mark on the rear plating of the first Volk. Armour buckled and sparks flew as the giant reeled from the unexpected attack. But Sova was slow, her movements uneven, and she struggled to keep her balance.

Just then, Katya decided to make her move.

Still undetected by the enemy, Katya moved with the calculated precision of a war machine designed for both battle and stealth. 'Engaging from behind,' she said calmly through the comms, her deep, steady voice at odds with the sudden burst of speed that propelled her across the open terrain. Inside the cockpit, Dimitri gripped the armrests, the vibrations from Katya's movement reverberating through his seat. He felt the sudden lurch as she accelerated.

The second Volk turned just in time to see Katya bearing down on it. Before it could react, Katya was upon it, her powerful limbs slamming into the machine's side, sending it off-balance. Dimitri rocked forward in his seat, the restraints holding him from battering against the window. The T90 fired wildly, but Katya ducked, her arm slamming into its damaged armour, the sound of screeching metal jarring.

While Katya engaged the second Volk, Sova staggered towards the first. Her cannons fired, but she was losing power fast. The first Volk turned, its cannons locking onto her damaged form. Rounds slammed into Sova's armour, knocking her off balance, but she refused to fall.

Dimitri clenched his fists, watching the battle unfold. 'Sova can't hold much longer!' he shouted into his comms piece.

Katya responded by driving her fist into the second Volk, her servos whirring as she shoved the enemy machine further off-balance. The T90 staggered, its heavy frame teetering. Before it could fully recover, a missile streaked from the Ukrainian trenches, cutting through the air and slamming into the back of the Volk's head. The explosion rocked the T90 as it crumpled to the ground, smoke billowing from the wreckage.

Katya stepped back, her targeting system locking onto Sova's opponent. 'Missiles locked,' she announced, and with a flash, a missile streaked through the air just as the Volk was about to bring its fist down on Sova. The Volk fell backwards from the explosion, which tore apart its chest before its legs gave way.

Without warning, Katya's sensors flared. Her voice broke through the silence, calm but urgent. 'Dimitri, incoming. Viper drone. Fast approach from the north.'

Dimitri's pulse quickened as he glanced at the display. A Viper drone was speeding towards them, cutting through the air above the treeline where they'd just been, like a deadly arrow.

'We need to take it down!' Dimitri shouted, his voice steady but filled with urgency.

'Agreed. I am preparing to engage with my cannons,' Katya replied, her servos revving.

Dimitri remembered the lessons Maksym had taught him only hours before. 'Wait! Let me take control of the cannons,' he said, gripping the controls in front of him.

There was a brief pause as Katya processed the request, before her voice came back, calm as ever. 'Understood. Cannons transferring to manual control. Good luck, Dimitri.'

The interface in front of Dimitri shifted as the controls for Katya's cannons materialised, identical to the ones in Sova's cockpit. He took a deep breath, his mind flashing back to the simulation. This was real now. He couldn't afford to miss.

The Viper was closing in fast, darting between the trees with lethal precision. Dimitri's hands trembled as he tracked it through the targeting system. He had to remember Maksym's advice: Don't chase it. Lead the shot.

'Dimitri, my boy, you've got this,' crackled Maksym over the comms, who was observing from his place in the treeline.

The drone zigzagged, too fast for him to keep up if he reacted to every movement. Dimitri gritted his teeth, waiting for the right moment. The Viper banked left, just like in the sim, and Dimitri adjusted the cannon's aim slightly ahead of its path.

He squeezed the trigger.

The cannon's fire reverberated through the cockpit, the shot streaking towards the Viper. For a split second, he thought he'd missed again, but then the blast clipped the drone's nose. The Viper lurched from the impact, trailing smoke as it spiralled towards the ground.

Dimitri barely had time to register what had happened before the Viper crashed into the trees with an explosion of sparks and debris.

Katya's voice broke through the ringing in Dimitri's ears. 'Viper neutralized. Excellent shot, Dimitri.'

Dimitri exhaled, a shaky smile breaking across his face. 'I … I did it,' he said, still processing the rush of adrenaline.

'Nice shot kid,' Maksym added through the comms, his tone calm but approving.

Dimitri hands slowly relaxed on the controls. He had done it – he had taken control, used what he'd learned, and brought down the threat.

The battlefield fell silent, the wreckage of the Volks smouldering. Sova, barely standing, limped forward.

Ukrainian soldiers, emboldened by the destruction of the Rusviet machines, surged from the trenches. A few Velociraptors, who had been hiding further away in the treeline, waiting for the T90s to breach the trenches, began to retreat under heavy fire. Resistance fighters targeted them with missiles and grenades, catching a few in fiery explosions before the rest slipped away into the shadows of the forest.

A figure emerged from the trench, his presence commanding the attention of everyone around. His battle-worn face was lined with experience, yet his gaze was sharp, taking in the aftermath of the battle with a quick, assessing glance.

'You must be the commander of this section,' Maksym observed as he walked over the open terrain to where Katya stood.

The commander gave a nod, acknowledging Maksym. 'Good timing for your team to turn up, especially your big friends.' He glanced towards Sova and Katya. 'We thank you for that. Without you, we'd still be pinned down.'

'Commander Ihor Kovalenko,' he introduced himself, extending a hand. His grip was firm, a mark of someone who had seen countless battles

Maksym didn't waste time with formalities. 'We're heading west,' he said, his voice tight with urgency. 'We need to reach Lviv.'

Kovalenko's expression darkened as his eyes shifted towards the horizon, where the twilight haze hung over the ruins. 'Lviv is still standing, but barely. The city's the last stronghold. The Rusviets are hitting it day and night. We've thrown everything we have at holding the line, but if they break through … it's over. For all of us.'

Maksym's jaw clenched at the weight of the commander's words. He glanced at Sova, her battered frame smoking. They had to keep moving, but it was clear Sova wouldn't make the journey in her current state.

Sensing Maksym's concern, the commander's expression softened. 'Before you go, I need to show you something,' he said, gesturing towards the base of operations nearby. 'We have a mobile repair station just beyond the trenches. We've salvaged enough parts from previous battles – we might be able to give your friend here some much-needed attention before you move on.'

Maksym exchanged glances with Dimitri. 'You're offering to repair Sova?' Dimitri asked, his voice tinged with both hope and disbelief.

Kovalenko nodded. 'She fought for us. It's the least we can do. We'll do what we can to get her operational, but it won't be easy. You'll need all the strength you can get before heading to Lviv.'

Maksym hesitated for only a moment. 'How long will it take?'

'Not long if my crew gets to work right away,' the commander assured. 'We're experts at makeshift repairs – done it enough times over the last few years.'

Maksym exhaled, feeling the weight of the decision. 'All right. Get to it.'

Kovalenko motioned for his team to move, and within minutes, a group of mechanics swarmed around Sova, assessing the damage. Katya stood nearby, watching silently. Dimitri and Maksym stepped back, giving the crew space as they worked.

'They'll get her up and running again,' the commander said, standing beside Maksym as the repairs began. 'It won't be perfect, but she'll be ready for what's ahead.'

Maksym nodded, grateful for the unexpected help. 'We'll need all the help we can get.'

The commander nodded. 'I might just need a little help in return.'

Chapter 11 – Steel Works

Kovalenko, a grizzled man with sharp eyes and a face hardened by years of battle, gestured towards a large map pinned to the wall of his dimly lit command centre, hidden just behind the main trench line. His finger traced a path along a marked area labelled *Steel Works*.

'We have a problem,' he began, his tone grim as his gaze shifted between Maksym and Dimitri. 'The Rusviets are holding a half-strength company of our soldiers as POWs in an old, abandoned Steel Works, about five kilometres from here. It's no doubt fortified, and we need to know what we're up against if we're going to make any progress in saving them.'

Maksym leaned forward, his eyes narrowing. 'What kind of fortifications are we talking about?'

The commander's jaw tightened. 'We don't know all the details yet. Our scouts haven't made it close enough. What we do know is they've stationed Velociraptors in the area. Ground patrols, drones, the works. We need someone to go in, find out what their defences look like, and report back. We can't move forward blind.'

Dimitri stood beside Maksym, listening intently. Maksym, however, wasn't convinced. His arms crossed over his chest, his instincts telling him there was more to this mission than simple reconnaissance.

'You're asking me to walk into a hornet's nest. I'll need more than just my team.'

Kovalenko hesitated, pretending to consider his options. 'I can spare you two A12 Sentinels,' he finally offered. 'They'll be enough for stealth and backup if things go sideways.'

Maksym raised an eyebrow, his suspicion deepening. 'Two? That's it?'

The commander gave a solemn nod. 'That's all I can spare right now. But trust me, they'll be more than enough for a recon mission.'

Maksym didn't respond immediately, his mind racing as he calculated the risks. Two Sentinels would be useful, but he knew the danger lurking at the abandoned Steel Works could be far greater than the commander was admitting. But with Lviv's survival hanging in the balance, they didn't have much choice.

After a long pause, Maksym gave a sharp nod. 'All right. We'll get your intel. But if this goes south, I want you to know we're coming back to settle the score.'

The commander's face softened into a faint, calculating smile. 'Just get me the information. The rest will follow.'

Kovalenko whistled, and two towering figures stepped in. The A12 Sentinels. Though relatively tall for humanoids, their black, gleaming exoskeletons made them appear even more menacing. As they approached, the first one – its visor gleaming with a blue light – tilted its head towards Maksym and cracked what could only be described as a robotic grin.

'We heard you needed the best, huh?' the first Sentinel quipped, amused. 'Well, here we are. Don't let the sleek look fool you. We've got enough firepower to take down a small city block.'

The second Sentinel chimed in, equally irreverent. 'And let's not forget, we come with a lifetime warranty. Any damage, we fix ourselves. You're in good hands.'

Maksym shot them both a look, but the banter continued as if they were a pair of well-oiled comedians instead of elite war machines.

'Look at this one,' the first Sentinel nodded towards Dimitri. 'Is this the pilot? He looks like he could use a protein shake.'

Dimitri blinked, unsure how to respond. Maksym pinched the bridge of his nose, already regretting the decision.

'They're better in combat,' the commander reassured, his voice deadpan, trying to hide a smirk. 'Or so I've been told.'

'Combat?' The second Sentinel flexed its metal fingers. 'That's our day job. Banter is our passion.'

Maksym grunted. 'Just don't get in my way.'

As they prepared to leave, the commander leaned in one last time, his eyes fixed on Maksym. 'Sova will need to rest following her serious repairs, and Dimitri can stay back to keep her company. Katya will be a valuable asset to help shore up our defences. We need all the help we can get.'

Maksym nodded, casting a glance at Dimitri, who seemed relieved at the idea of staying with Sova. The machine was in rough shape, her systems strained from the previous battle. A deep repair cycle was exactly what she needed if they were going to push forward later.

'You'll go with the two Sentinels for recon,' Kovalenko continued. 'Find out what's happening at the Steel Works, then report back. It's crucial for us to know what kind of defences we're up against. Time's running out, and we need to be prepared for whatever the Rusviets throw at us.'

Maksym didn't respond immediately, his jaw tightening as he considered the task ahead. Leaving Sova behind wasn't ideal, but he knew she wouldn't make it far in her current state. At least Dimitri would be with her.

'Good luck,' the commander added, his tone grave. 'And remember, our survival depends on that intel. Get it, and we might stand a chance.'

Maksym nodded again, feeling the weight of responsibility settle on his shoulders. As he left the command centre, both Sentinels flanking him, he couldn't shake the feeling that something was off, a nagging sense of unease creeping into the back of his mind. But he pushed it aside – there was no room for doubt now.

'Dimitri, take care of Sova while she rests,' Maksym said. His mind already raced over what he might encounter in the reconnaissance. He held a map of the Steel Works, considering various ways to get close without being detected.

The journey to the abandoned Steel Works started under a gloomy sky, the dense clouds overhead adding a sense of unease to the mission. Maksym and the two A12 Sentinels moved swiftly ahead through the trees, their footfalls barely audible on the forest floor. Dimitri lingered behind, his gaze constantly drifting back to Sova, who had powered down for a necessary Deep Sleep. Her systems needed time to recover after the strain of recent battles, and the quiet hum from her idle state was the only sign of life.

'She'll be out for a while,' Dimitri muttered, running his hand along the cool, dormant metal of Sova's cockpit. Despite her imposing presence, Sova looked vulnerable at rest, her large frame having been moved into an even larger tent for repairs.

'Dimitri,' came Kovalenko's voice, breaking the silence. He approached with an air of authority, his face shadowed by concern. 'We need to talk.'

Dimitri turned to face him, his instincts on edge. 'What is it?'

The commander's gaze flicked towards Sova, then back to Dimitri. 'Maksym has requested you join him on the way to the Steel Works,' he said, his voice calm but urgent. 'He believes your nimble frame can help them. You won't be involved in any combat, just acting as recon.'

Dimitri frowned. 'But Maksym told me to stay here, with Sova, in case something happens.'

'That was before,' Kovalenko replied smoothly. 'He didn't anticipate the difficulty they might face getting into the Steel Works. We need every advantage we can get, and you might be able to help. Besides, Sova's in Deep Sleep while under repairs – she won't wake for hours, and we can't afford to wait.'

Dimitri hesitated. He glanced at Sova again – her armour, once smooth and gleaming, was now pockmarked with deep gashes and scorch marks. Parts of her outer plating hung loose, exposing the intricate systems beneath.

A team of repair technicians swarmed around her, their welding torches sparking as they worked frantically to repair her damaged hull. The air under the tent canopy was filled with the steady rhythm of tools clanking against metal, and the hiss of welding flames as they tried to patch up Sova's breaches. Hydraulic fluid seeped from a few broken joints, pooling beneath her as the crew worked to replace the damaged lines.

At the heart of the operation, towering over everyone, was Katya. The former Rusviet engineer worked swiftly and efficiently, her arm extending tools with ease. She moved with practiced precision, using her knowledge of war machines to assist the team in repairing the critical systems. From time to time, she barked out orders to the technicians in clipped tones, directing them to focus on key areas that needed immediate attention.

'Reinforce her chest plate, here!' Katya ordered, pointing to a section of Sova's armour that had taken heavy fire. 'And get the power cells connected – she needs full energy flow to reboot!'

With her arm's mechanical appendage, she accessed Sova's internal systems, running diagnostics on her core processor. Lights blinked weakly from within Sova's frame, indicators showing which systems were operational and which were failing. The repair was a race against time, but Katya's presence gave them hope – her intimate knowledge of repairing machines made her indispensable.

One of the technicians stepped back, wiping sweat from his brow. 'We're getting there,' he said, though his tone was strained. 'She'll be operational soon, but she's not at full strength.'

Katya paused, towering over the technicians as she caught Dimitri's hesitation. 'She'll be fine,' Katya said, her voice carrying a surprising warmth, despite the timbre of her speech. She crouched down to meet Dimitri's gaze, her large arm resting carefully beside him. 'I'll make sure of it.'

The ground trembled beneath her as she adjusted, her weight heavier than usual from the engineering-grade equipment she carried in her right arm.

Dimitri nodded, but the enormity of the decision hung over him. His hand lingered on Sova's cool metal surface for a moment longer, as if he could will her back to full power just by being there. But Katya's words, and the quiet buzz of repair work, gave him some peace.

Reluctantly, Dimitri nodded. 'Alright … but what if something happens to Sova while I'm gone?'

The commander's lips twitched. 'Don't worry about Sova,' he said, placing a reassuring hand on Dimitri's shoulder. 'I'll keep an eye on her myself. You focus on the mission.'

Dimitri gave one last uncertain look at Sova before following Kovalenko towards the group of soldiers waiting nearby. The small squad led him deeper into the forest, the trees closing in around them as they moved further from Sova's resting place. The commander walked at the rear, his expression unreadable, but Dimitri couldn't shake the feeling that something was wrong.

After an hour of traveling through the forest, the abandoned Steel Works loomed ahead, an industrial fortress of rusting metal and towering chimneys. Smoke rose from its vents like a warning, and the air grew thick with the scent of oil and decay. The soldiers slowed as they neared the old railway track leading into the complex, but it wasn't the sight of the Steel Works that made Dimitri's stomach turn – it was the eerie silence that followed.

As they approached the outskirts of the facility, one of the soldiers moved deliberately towards the rear, close to where Kovalenko walked. Without warning, the soldier made a subtle motion, slipping his hand to his belt to trigger something Dimitri couldn't see.

Suddenly, the distant sound of S10 Velociraptors echoed from within the Steel Works – their clanking metal limbs growing louder by the second.

Dimitri's heart raced as he spun towards the commander, eyes wide with panic. 'What's going on? Why would they—'

Before he could finish, the soldiers seized him by the arms, dragging him off the path and into a nearby clearing.

'Let me go!' Dimitri shouted, trying to pull free. 'What are you doing?'

Kovalenko finally spoke, his voice cold and calculating. 'I'm afraid you've outlived your usefulness, Dimitri. Sova's too valuable to be left in the hands of a child.'

Dimitri's mind reeled. 'What are you talking about? You said—'

'I said a lot of things,' the commander cut in sharply. 'But the truth is, Sova needs a real pilot, not a crippled boy. Someone with experience, someone who can lead our forces and hold the line against the Rusviets. You've done well enough to keep her operational, but you don't have the skills to win this war.'

Realization dawned on Dimitri, and his blood ran cold. 'You're going to wipe her memory … and take her for yourself.'

Kovalenko nodded slowly, an almost pitying look in his eyes. 'It's nothing personal. Sova is too important to risk with just anyone. Once she's been reset, I'll take command of her, and we'll have a fighting chance.'

Dimitri's heart pounded in his chest, fury and fear mixing in a rush of adrenaline. 'You won't get away with this!'

'Oh, but I already have,' Kovalenko replied, signalling to the soldiers. 'Take him. I'll deal with Sova myself.'

As the soldiers tied Dimitri to a nearby tree and then quietly slipped away into the forest, the sound of Velociraptors could be heard closing in. With his men walking before him, the commander turned and strode back towards the forest – towards Sova, still in her vulnerable Deep Sleep.

Dimitri struggled against the ropes binding him to the tree, the rough fibres cutting into his wrists. His heart pounded as he glanced through the dense forest, hoping to catch sight of Maksym or anyone coming to his rescue. But the forest remained silent, save for the occasional rustle of leaves in the cold wind.

He wasn't sure how long he'd been tied there, but every second felt like an eternity. The commander's betrayal still echoed in his mind – Sova was in danger, and he was powerless to stop it.

A low hum reached his ears, growing louder with each passing moment. Dimitri's pulse quickened.

The Velociraptors appeared in the clearing, their sleek bodies moving with a predatory grace.

One of the Velociraptors tilted its head as it scanned Dimitri. A brief whirring sound followed, and then, without a word, one of the machines extended a sharp claw, swiftly cutting through the ropes that bound him.

Dimitri stumbled forward, free but unsteady, rubbing his sore wrists. He shot a wary glance at the machine, unsure if he should be relieved or terrified.

The lead Velociraptor spoke in a cold tone. 'You boy, you're coming with us.' It gestured for him to follow. Its claw pointed towards the looming silhouette of the Steel Works, visible through the thinning trees.

'No …' Dimitri muttered under his breath. He didn't want to go back there – he knew it was a trap. But with no other option, and the cold gaze of the Velociraptors fixed on him, he had no choice but to comply.

As he trudged forward, the two S10s flanked him on either side, their presence like an iron cage around him. His every movement was monitored, and escape was impossible.

From a distance, Maksym watched through his scope as an instantly recognisable slim boy with ruddy brown hair emerged from the treeline.

'What the hell?' Maksym muttered, lowering the scope slightly. Dimitri was walking towards the Steel Works, flanked by two Velociraptors.

'I thought the kid was supposed to be with Sova,' one of the Sentinels – Orlov – said, his voice tinged with concern.

Maksym frowned, his mind working through the scenario. 'He was.'

'Maybe he's just taking a scenic route,' Kirov, the other Sentinel, chimed in sarcastically. 'Could be a nice stroll through enemy-infested territory.'

'Yeah, nothing like a bit of fresh air when you're surrounded by machines that could snap your spine like a twig,' Orlov added with a grin. 'Real calming.'

Maksym's eyes narrowed as he watched the scene unfold. 'No … something's wrong. The commander told me Dimitri would stay behind with Sova. Why is he walking towards the Steel Works, guarded by those damn Velociraptors?'

Kirov snorted. 'Maybe Kovalenko's got his own plans. You know how these guys think – always about the bigger picture.'

Orlov shot a glance at Maksym. 'Could be a setup. You think the commander's playing us?'

Maksym didn't respond immediately, but his instincts screamed that Orlov was right. Kovalenko had been insistent about the importance of the mission, the reconnaissance, but now Dimitri was walking into the heart of enemy territory, seemingly under guard.

'I don't know yet,' Maksym finally replied, his tone grim. 'But I'm not leaving him to whatever mess this is.'

Kirov smirked, patting his oversized rifle. 'Well, looks like we get to play hero again. Never a dull day.'

Orlov chuckled. 'Right. Just another routine rescue mission, right after we stroll through a factory filled with feisty Velociraptors.'

Maksym shot them both a look, but despite their banter, he knew he could count on the Sentinels when it mattered. 'We'll need to move fast. The longer Dimitri's deep inside, the harder it'll be to get him out.'

Orlov shrugged, his joints whirring as he adjusted his position. 'Fast is our middle name, boss.'

'Speak for yourself,' Kirov added, 'Mine's 'careful.' Or 'handsome.' It depends on who you ask.'

'Save it,' Maksym snapped, already rising from his position. 'Let's get moving.'

The two Sentinels fell in beside him as they silently made their way down the hill towards the Steel Works. Though they maintained their banter, Maksym could sense the growing tension in the air. Time was running out for Dimitri – and for Sova.

Maksym paused at the edge of the treeline, squinting against the harsh daylight as he scanned the towering Steel Works structure ahead. The morning sun cast long shadows across the complex, but its glaring light made any movement even more visible. Velociraptor patrols moved along the perimeter, their sensors sweeping methodically across the open ground. Even in daylight, the Sentinels had already activated their cloaking suits, and though the sunlight gleamed off the rusting steel beams and crumbling walls, their forms were still imperceptible, blending with the industrial terrain.

The Velociraptor patrols continued their rounds in synchronized movements, oblivious to the Sentinels standing just within the treeline. Maksym glanced back at them, their figures hidden in plain sight thanks to their cloaking technology. The slight shimmer of their suits was nearly impossible to notice unless you knew exactly what to look for. In the daylight, it was a harder game, but their movements remained fluid and controlled, designed to avoid even the smallest reflection that might give them away.

Maksym scanned the compound again, focusing on the guards and the main gate ahead. His mind turned through possible approaches, and after a careful assessment, he pulled out his own cloaking suit to hide his heat signature, then gestured for the Sentinels to follow. The Sentinels moved without a sound, their Longbow rifles slung across their broad shoulders. Each rifle was capable of taking out heavy armour from a distance with its explosive impact, but here, stealth was paramount. Their short-barrelled, detachable miniguns, built for rapid suppression fire, remained secured for now. Designed to perch on their shoulders or fire autonomously from the ground, the guns could unleash a torrent of bullets in seconds.

The trio moved like predators through the overgrown grass, careful not to disturb the landscape and risk detection.

Maksym adjusted his grip on his automatic rifle, the short barrel aimed low as he moved silently towards the perimeter. The carbine's compact design was perfect for close-quarters combat, and the suppressor attached ensured that if things got tight, he could eliminate threats quietly. His pack, though lighter than usual without the missile launcher, was still equipped with extra magazines, recon gear, and essential supplies. The weight felt reassuring as he moved swiftly but silently.

Maksym could feel the heat of the sun through his suit, but he forced himself to focus. The drone of machinery in the distance and the hum of nearby surveillance drones added tension to the scene. From this distance, he could see that the Steel Works was heavily fortified, with guard towers positioned strategically and sensors positioned to cover nearly every angle. He motioned to the Sentinels to hold their position as another patrol passed, their footsteps echoing against the metal pathways that lined the compound.

Once the patrol moved out of view, Maksym scanned for a blind spot near the gate. The cloaking suits would hide them from the sensors, but the daylight made visibility from the guards a constant risk. He signalled to his companions, their movements ghostlike as they shifted closer to the gate.

Dropping to one knee behind a stack of discarded metal beams, Maksym watched the guards intently. The heat haze rising from the ground warped the air slightly, but he could still make out the soldiers, their weapons at the ready. His eyes darted between the guards and the looming structure ahead.

'Wait for the patrol to move behind the south tower,' Maksym said quietly into his comms, his voice steady despite the tension. 'When the angle's clear, we move. No unnecessary risks. We get in, we scout and find Dimitri, and we leave. Minimal contact.'

The Sentinels, their weapons held steady, gave subtle nods.

Maksym's muscles tensed as the next patrol began to move. The sunlight glinted off their titanium alloy frames, and the whir of their joints faded as they rounded the corner behind the south tower. Maksym gestured sharply, and they moved – silent shadows under the blinding sun.

'We need to time this just right,' Maksym whispered. 'When the next patrol passes, we slip through the gate.'

Kirov, in a deadpan tone, remarked, 'I've calculated a 92% chance we can make it without triggering the alarms. The other 8% involves heavy gunfire and probable dismemberment. Let's aim for the 92%, shall we?'

Maksym suppressed a grin as he crouched waiting for the perfect moment. The Velociraptor patrol marched past, disappearing from view. With a quick hand signal, he sprinted forward, the Sentinels flanking him as they slipped past the gate and toward the shadowed wall of the building. The abandoned Steel Works was old, and the infrastructure was riddled with access points. Orlov was first to reach the rusted service door. Extending both arms, he gripped the edge of the frame and tugged. Old hinges, rusted with age, gave way with a minimal screech. With the door carefully pulled back into position, minus the broken hinges, the trio slipped into the dark maintenance corridor, disappearing just as the next patrol rounded the corner.

The inside of the abandoned facility was a maze of metal and industrial piping, the air thick with heat and the muffled drone of machinery.
The Sentinels moved in silence, scanning their surroundings with advanced sensor arrays. Their bodies glided over the floor of the corridors, tracking the heat signatures left by Dimitri. The trail was fragmented, but it was enough.

'His captors are using the east corridor,' Kirov muttered. 'I'll go ahead and scout, see if I can find him.'

The shadows seemed to close in on Dimitri as his guards guided him deeper into the labyrinth of corridors. Their slim frames loomed over him, moving with a fluid grace that made his skin crawl.

As they moved deeper, Dimitri caught snippets of a conversation between the two Velociraptors. Their voices were subdued and distorted by static, but their words were clear.

'The final assault is set for tomorrow at dawn,' one rasped, its voice a mix of hard clicks and guttural tones. 'The Red Guards will advance first, soften the defences. Then we sweep in, as always.'

The second Velociraptor nodded, its head tilting, eyes glowing with a red hue. 'They say the resistance is faltering. Lviv's defences are weaker than expected – crumbling like all the others.'

'Yes, but the High Commissariat demands total eradication,' the first one replied, an edge of eagerness creeping into its voice. 'No survivors this time. The order is absolute.'

Dimitri's heart skipped a beat. Lviv. They were going to strike at dawn. He tried to keep his expression neutral, but his thoughts spiralled with urgency. He had to get out. He had to warn Maksym before it was too late.

Suddenly, an audible clatter reverberated from somewhere deeper in the building – a distinct noise that cut through the Velociraptors' conversation. Both machines froze, their heads swivelling in unison, sensors flaring to life. Dimitri held his breath, his heart pounding against his ribs. The air was thick with tension, the only sound the purr of the Velociraptors' systems.

Rounding the corner of the passage from behind them, Kirov casually strolled into view, as if he had all the time in the world. His tall, human-sized frame seemed impossibly relaxed given the deadly machines standing just meters away. The grin on his face was unmistakable.

'Hey, Dimitri!' Kirov called out, voice full of false cheer. 'You're needed back at camp. Maksym says you forgot to feed the dog or something.'

The Velociraptors snapped to attention, their miniguns whirring to life as their systems identified the threat.

Before they could react, Kirov was already moving. With lightning speed, he brought up his massive rifle, letting loose a barrage of high-velocity rounds. The first impact exploded with a large bang and flash, crumpling the guard immediately to Dimitri's right, sparks flying from its chassis as the explosive round tore through its armour like paper.

The second Velociraptor opened fire, a hail of bullets cutting through the air. Kirov barely flinched as he charged forward, using his own body as a shield. Several rounds impacted his frame, leaving scorched dents in his armour, but he didn't slow down.

Kirov returned fire, whizzing past Dimitri's crouched frame by no more than a centimetre, The shot connected with the Velociraptor, its steel frame shuddering violently as the explosion ripped through it, tearing its head clean off its shoulders in a shower of sparks and twisted steel.

The firefight had ended as abruptly as it had begun, leaving the corridor littered with the smouldering remains of both S10s. Kirov stood in the centre, smoke rising from his battered frame, still grinning despite the damage he'd taken.

'Phew, that was close,' Kirov said with a wink, though his tone carried some concern. 'Didn't think I'd have to work this hard today.'

Dimitri, still in shock, nodded numbly. His ears were ringing from the firefight, but he could hear it – the unmistakable sound of more Velociraptors approaching. Their footsteps echoed down the corridor, growing louder by the second.

'Kirov, we need to move. Now,' Maksym's voice carried from another corridor. A moment later, Maksym and Orlov emerged from the shadows of a side passage, weapons drawn.

'More on the way,' Maksym warned, eyes sharp. 'This way.'

Without a word, Kirov nodded and ushered Dimitri towards Maksym. The boy's legs were shaky, but Kirov kept a firm hand on his shoulder, guiding him through the narrow passage as the sound of the approaching machines grew louder.

Orlov gave Kirov a sideways glance. 'You look like you've had better days, my friend.'

Kirov chuckled. 'You should see the other guys.'

'Yeah, I saw them,' Orlov replied with a smirk. 'They're scrap metal now.'

'Focus,' Maksym snapped, leading them down a side corridor. The air was thick with tension as the sound of the S10s drew closer.

'Keep close,' Maksym added. 'We're not out of this yet.' He led the group deeper into the Steel Works. His sharp eyes scanned the environment, assessing their options, but the path ahead was rapidly narrowing.

They reached a dead end.

'Dammit,' Maksym muttered under his breath, flicking open his map in a desperate bid to find a way out. The blueprints of the abandoned Steel Works flickered in the diffuse light as his fingers traced the routes. He forced himself to stay calm. They were boxed in, and the enemy was closing fast.

Dimitri glanced nervously back down the corridor where they had just come from. The clanking of the approaching machines grew louder. The Sentinels stood ready, their weapons drawn, scanning the area for an ambush.

Then Maksym's head snapped upward, eyes narrowing as he spotted something – a service duct, almost hidden behind a rusted grate.

'There!' Maksym barked, pointing towards it. 'That's our way out.'

Kirov looked up at the small duct, then at Dimitri and the others. He grinned, his typical good-natured humour shining through even in the dire situation.

'Well, looks like my job just got exciting,' Kirov said, swinging his MGX-40 Minigun off his back and placing it on the ground. 'I'll hold them off here. You three, get up there and get moving.'

'Kirov—' Dimitri began, but Kirov waved him off, still smiling.

'Don't worry, kid. I've faced worse. Just keep moving, and I'll make sure they don't follow.'

Maksym didn't hesitate. He grabbed the grate and pulled it off with a sharp tug, revealing the small duct behind it. 'Go!' he ordered, shoving Dimitri forward. The boy scrambled up first, using the walls to boost himself into the narrow tunnel. Orlov followed, then Maksym.

Down below, Kirov knelt beside his Minigun, giving it a reassuring pat, then turned towards the mouth of the corridor as the sound of the approaching S10s reached a fever pitch.

'They're here,' Orlov whispered from within the duct, his voice tense as they crawled through the cramped space.

Kirov's grin widened as he heard the clicking and clanking of the S10s around the corner. He activated his autocannon, the weapon spinning to life, and took a deep breath.

'All right, boys,' he muttered to himself, watching the shadows stretch as the S10s approached. 'Let's dance.'

The first trio of Velociraptors rounded the corner, their sensors locking onto Kirov instantly. They raised their guns, but Kirov was faster. He unleashed a hail of fire from his autocannon, the heavy rounds tearing into the lead S10's chest before it could even open fire. Sparks flew, and the machine staggered backwards, collapsing into a heap of twisted metal.

But the other two pressed on, their miniguns whirring to life. Kirov ducked behind a pillar just as a torrent of bullets rained down where he had been standing. He gritted his teeth, feeling the impact of rounds hitting the pillar near his head.

'You're gonna have to do better than that!' Kirov shouted, popping out to return fire. His rounds hit one of the remaining Velociraptors in the leg, sending it crashing to the floor, its limbs thrashing wildly.

The third Velociraptor charged forward, twin miniguns spitting a relentless hail of bullets. Sparks erupted across Kirov's armour as he braced, quickly switching to his rifle as the machine closed in. At the last second, he sidestepped, pivoting to unload a barrage into its flank. The impact sent the S10 staggering, but not before its own rounds tore into Kirov's shoulder.

Kirov spun around from the impact, but he didn't slow down. With one final shot, he took down the last Velociraptor, its body crashing to the ground in a smoking heap.

Inside the duct, Maksym, Dimitri, and Orlov could hear the battle raging below. The sound of gunfire and metal clashing echoed through the narrow passage, but they pressed on, moving as quickly as they could through the confined space.

'Kirov's buying us time,' Maksym muttered. 'We need to move faster.'

From below, the distant sound of more Velociraptors could be heard, their reinforcements arriving. Dimitri's heart sank as he realized how many there were. He didn't want to leave Kirov behind, but he knew they didn't have a choice.

'Kirov's a damn fool,' Orlov whispered, but there was an unmistakable respect in his voice.

The trio pressed on through the narrow service duct, Maksym leading the way with the map unfolded in one hand, its glow illuminating the path ahead. The bustle of machinery and distant clanking of S10s echoed all around, but Maksym remained focused, eyes darting between the map and their surroundings.

'Keep moving,' Maksym hissed. 'We're almost over it.'

'Over what?' Dimitri asked.

Maksym didn't answer. As they reached a grate below, Maksym held up his hand to signal a stop. Beneath them was a large, high-tech room, filled with glowing screens and war maps of Ukraine projected on walls. AI commanders gathered around tables and terminals, plans meticulously spread out before them.

'Rusviet command and control,' Maksym whispered, a grim smile crossing his face. 'No wonder they've got so many Velociraptors patrolling this place.'

Orlov peeked through the grate. 'We can't pass this up.'

'No, we can't,' Maksym replied, pulling out his rifle. 'On my mark.'

Peering through the narrow slats of the grate, Maksym's eyes locked onto the Rusviet AI commanders gathered below. Their tall, angular forms stood around a holographic map of Lviv, the red and blue icons flickering with every tactical update. Dimitri stayed back, keeping his breath shallow and silent, while Orlov positioned himself beside Maksym, weapon at the ready.

'Wait,' Maksym whispered, holding up a hand as he leaned closer, straining to catch every word from the commanders below.

The monotone voices of the commanders clicked and whirred, their speech stiff and deliberate. 'The dawn assault will commence as planned,' one intoned. 'The Signals Drone will deploy from the castle ruins, transmitting orders to all units in the sector.'

'The Red Guards will engage first, drawing out any remaining resistance,' another chimed in. 'Once they are exposed, the Volkov T90s will advance. Lviv must fall by midday.'

Maksym's jaw tightened. This was it – their entire attack strategy laid out in front of them. But before he could signal to Orlov, something new caught his eye. Emerging from the shadows at the edge of the chamber was a figure unlike any other he had seen.

A High Commissariat Commander.

The man strode forward with a deliberate, authoritative gait, his presence commanding the entire room. He was old – greying at the temples with lines of experience etched into his weathered face – but there was nothing frail about him. His posture was straight, his shoulders broad, and the way he carried himself spoke of a lifetime spent at the highest echelons of power. His uniform, sleek and dark, was devoid of any unnecessary embellishments, but it reflected the sheer authority he wielded. Every step he took radiated control, as though the very air around him bent to his will.

What made him even more striking, however, was the figure at his side – a Velociraptor, but unlike the others Maksym had encountered. This one was a deep, polished black, its armoured plating glossier and more refined. It moved with a sinister, elegance, its joints silent, its red optics glowing brighter than those of its counterparts. The Velociraptor stayed close to the Commander's side, flanking him like a shadow, its movements as cold and deliberate as the man it guarded.

Maksym watched the Commander with a mixture of awe and dread. This man wasn't just another leader – he was someone who could change the tide of battle with a single command. His very presence seemed to shift the atmosphere in the room, as though everyone else were merely pieces on a chessboard, awaiting his next move.

Everyone fell silent as the High Commissariat Commander approached the holographic map. His gaze swept over the display with cold calculation. 'The final assault on Lviv must not fail,' his voice dripped with authority. 'I've come to ensure that it doesn't.'

Maksym exchanged a glance with Orlov, who nodded, understanding the gravity of what they were witnessing. This wasn't just an attack – it was the final push to take Lviv, and the presence of a High Commissariat Commander meant the stakes were even higher than they'd realised.

They needed to get that data – now more than ever.

'Hold position,' Maksym whispered, eyes fixed on the door at the far end of the command room. The tension in the air was palpable as the High Commissariat Commander stood, his gaze sweeping over the room one last time. The AI commanders, though expressionless, seemed to brace themselves for his departure. The High Commander straightened his coat, then turned sharply, his imposing form making its way towards the door. The room seemed to collectively exhale as his footsteps echoed on the cold metal floor, the rhythmic sound gradually fading into the distance.

The Rusviet commanders, still standing at attention, showed a subtle but noticeable shift in their posture. An almost imperceptible sense of relief rippled through them. Their heads swivelled as they turned towards the door, and one by one, they followed the High Commander, their movements more fluid, less rigid than before. The sound of their footsteps reverberated in the corridor, growing fainter until silence filled the room once more.

'Now,' Maksym hissed. He and Orlov moved swiftly, prying open the grate and dropping silently into the room below.

Every second counted. Maksym moved swiftly to the command console, his fingers hovering over the controls, but he hesitated for a moment, glancing at Orlov.

'Did you catch it?' Maksym whispered, his voice tense.

Orlov nodded, his eyes locked on the console. 'I saw the commander input the codes. It was fast, but I've got it.' He quickly rattled off the sequence.

Maksym's fingers flew across the console, entering the codes Orlov had memorised. The system responded immediately, granting him access to the orders for the Signals Drone. The console lit up as the transmission orders appeared on the screen.

'Perfect,' Maksym muttered under his breath as he pulled out a small data drive and inserted it into the terminal. The download initiated, the percentage ticking up slowly as the critical data transferred. Every second felt like an eternity.

'Hurry up,' Orlov urged quietly, casting quick glances towards the door. The faraway glow of the AI commanders' eyes was visible once again, their patrols bringing them closer.

Maksym didn't flinch, his focus unwavering. 'Almost there …' He watched as the data transfer climbed – 85%, 92%, 100%. As soon as the download was complete, Maksym yanked the drive from the console, slipping it securely into his vest.

Maksym stood beneath the grate, still a few feet above his head. Without missing a beat, Orlov moved over and hoisted Maksym up. Maksym grabbed the edges of the grate and pulled himself through with a swift, fluid motion.

Orlov crouched low, gathering his strength, then leapt upward with impressive power. He cleared the distance effortlessly, catching the edge of the opening and pulling himself through, landing silently beside Maksym.

They moved back to the grate, their exit as silent as their entry.

Just as they secured the grate back in place, the door to the command room slid open, and the commanders re-entered, oblivious to the intrusion. Maksym exhaled, his heart pounding in his ears as he and Orlov exchanged a brief look of triumph.

'Got it,' Maksym mouthed to Dimitri, who nodded, relieved. They had what they needed. Now they just had to get this information to Lviv before it was too late.

Without another word, they began to scramble through the ducts, moving as fast as they could while crouched low. The ducts groaned under their weight as they raced against time, every second precious.

They half expected alarms to sound as a result of the gun battle between Kirov and the Velociraptors, but thankfully they heard nothing yet.

'Faster!' Maksym urged, his eyes scanning the map for the nearest exit. The ducts twisted and turned, but Maksym's instincts guided them.

The air was tense, and the urgency of their situation gnawed at Dimitri's nerves. He could hear Orlov behind him, the adrenaline pushing them all forward.

'Here!' Maksym whispered urgently, pointing to a panel just ahead. He moved quickly, inspecting the area for any surveillance. After a brief pause, he kicked the panel open.

One by one, they dropped silently out of the duct, landing on the rough terrain outside the Steel Works. Maksym's eyes scanned their surroundings immediately for activity. They crouched low behind a stack of rusted beams, waiting for the patrol to pass.

The hum of nearby drones echoed through the air, and Maksym signalled for Orlov and Dimitri to stay hidden. After a tense moment, the patrol moved on, and Maksym motioned for the group to follow.

As they were about to disappear into the cover of the forest, a deep rumble caught their attention. A large craft, streamlined and dark, was lifting off from a platform at the far side of the Steel Works. Its massive engines pulsed, and it ascended steadily, hovering above the complex for a moment before angling towards the east.

Dimitri noticed the insignia emblazoned on the craft's side – a gleaming red star, encircled by the black crest of the High Commissariat. It was unmistakable.

'Well, look who decided to show up – just in time for lunch.' Orlov spoke excitedly.

Dimitri spun around, eyes widening as Kirov staggered out from between the trees, his metal body battered, shredded in parts, sparks flickering across the torn edges of his armour. He was limping badly, but still somehow managed to grin through his injuries.

'Kirov!' Orlov gasped, rushing over to his fellow Sentinel.

Kirov waved him off with a good-natured chuckle, despite the clear damage to his frame. 'I told you I'd hold them off. Just, uh … didn't expect them to be so determined. I even managed to stuff their broken frames into the ventilation shaft, hopefully they won't be missed too much.

'You're not gonna miss lunch, are you?' Maksym replied, his voice carrying an edge of relief, but he didn't miss a beat as he checked Kirov's damaged body. 'You're in rough shape, though. Let's get you fixed up.'

Kirov shrugged, his humour still intact. 'I'm fine. Don't worry about me. Just needed a little workout.'

Maksym's face hardened as he motioned for the group to move. 'We need to get to Sova.'

They moved swiftly through the forest. The memory of the Commander's cryptic plans gnawed at Maksym, and the thought of Sova being tampered with sent a chill down Dimitri's spine.

When they reached the station where they had left Sova, a cold fury settled in Maksym's gut. The repair bay, once bustling with activity, now stood deserted. The technicians and Katya were gone, leaving behind scattered tools, diagnostic screens still glowing faintly, and half-repaired components. The air was thick with the scent of oil and burned metal, the emptiness of the place cold with betrayal.

Sova crouched in the centre of the bay, her panels removed to expose vital systems. Her cockpit lay open, vulnerable, and unprotected – something Dimitri had left unattended, trusting that no one would dare approach her in such a state.

There, standing next to Sova, was Kovalenko. His tall figure was bent over the cockpit, his hand gripping a long probe. The instrument hovered just above the exposed controls, poised to begin the reprogramming process. His expression was one of grim determination, as if he were about to take a necessary step, regardless of the cost.

Dimitri's blood ran cold as the scene unfolded before him. He had left the cockpit exposed, never thinking anyone would dare interfere with Sova while she was being repaired. Kovalenko, once an ally, now stood on the verge of taking matters into his own hands, ready to overwrite Sova's programming without consulting them.

Kovalenko froze as they emerged from the trees, his expression shifting from surprise to frustration. 'Stop right there!' he shouted, his voice trembling with barely restrained anger. 'This wasn't what it looks like.'

Maksym stepped forward, his eyes locked on the Commander, voice as cold as steel. 'I'd suggest you think very carefully about your next move.'

Kovalenko's face twisted, his hand still hovering near the probe. 'I had no choice! You don't understand – if we don't use Sova, we'll lose everything! My men, the defence line, the whole region – this was just to save my troops!'

Dimitri stepped closer, his gaze focused on the Commander. 'You were going to wipe her memory,' he said quietly. It was a statement – not a question.

Kovalenko's rage flickered, his shoulders sagging as the truth settled in. 'We needed her. You don't know what it's like, watching everything you've built fall apart knowing that this machine could turn the tide.'

Maksym's hand tightened on his weapon, but his voice was calm – dangerously so. 'Sova doesn't belong to you. She made her choice when she picked Dimitri.'

The Commander growled, lowering the probe slowly. 'I wasn't going to destroy her … just make sure she followed orders.'

'By wiping everything she knows?' Maksym took a step forward, his tone hardening. 'You're done here.'

Orlov, keeping his weapon trained on the Commander, spoke up, the banter still present in his voice despite the tension. 'Well, Kovalenko, I'd say it's about time you backed off. Can't have you getting in the way of Sova's nap.'

The Commander's hand finally dropped, his desperation palpable. 'I only wanted to give us a chance to survive ….'

'Then we'll do it the right way,' Maksym replied coldly. 'With Sova and Dimitri.'

Kirov, limping over despite his injuries, gave the Commander a good-natured pat on the back, his voice light. 'Cheer up, Commander. Lunch is still on, right?'

With the situation defused, the group hurried to Sova. Dimitri rushed to the cockpit, relieved to see that the

Commander hadn't yet activated the probe. As he reached to close it, he muttered, 'Sorry, Sova. Won't leave you open again.' Sova, still in Deep Sleep, did not reply.

Maksym turned to Kovalenko, his voice like iron. 'You're done here. Stay out of our way, or you'll wish you had.'

Kovalenko, defeated but still simmering, could only nod as Maksym and the others prepared to move out.

The second-in-command stepped forward, a stark contrast to the now-disgraced Commander. He was a tall, broad-shouldered man in his late thirties, with a square jaw covered in a light dusting of stubble. His short-cropped hair, the colour of ash, was streaked with the dirt and grime of the battlefield. His olive-green uniform bore the insignia of a seasoned officer, but his face showed a weariness that came from more than just lack of sleep. The weight of leadership had clearly shifted to him, but he bore it with a quiet, determined resolve.

Wiping sweat from his brow, he managed a weary smile and placed a firm hand on Maksym's shoulder. His eyes, though tired, gleamed with the sharpness of a man who had seen too much of war but refused to falter.

'You're Maksym, right?' the officer asked, his voice deep and calm despite the chaos around them. 'I'm Major

Mykola Veselov. It's my turn to keep this mess together now.'

Maksym nodded, sensing through the brief exchange the respect that the Major commanded from his troops. Veselov took a deep breath, glancing towards the horizon, where the distant rumble of artillery echoed from the front lines.

'When you reach the city,' Veselov began, his tone growing more serious, 'find General Kozak. He's organizing the defence in Lviv. Tell him you're with me, and …' His voice wavered, the weight of his words pressing heavily on him. 'Tell him to hold out as long as he can. Reinforcements are scarce, and the Rusviets are pushing hard.'

He tightened his grip on Maksym's shoulder, a silent show of solidarity, then released him. 'Some sections of the road to Lviv are dangerous – enemy forward patrols, aerial scans, the works. Stick to the forests; they might give you some cover until you're closer to the city.'

Veselov's gaze shifted to the two Sentinels, Kirov and Orlov, their tall, battle-worn frames standing like silent guardians in the dim light. Despite the scarring and battered armour, they still radiated strength, and for a moment, Veselov seemed to draw hope from their presence.

'Kirov, Orlov,' Veselov addressed them directly, 'you're not going to make it far in this state. Find a technician – get those repairs done.' He paused. 'In fact, I want you two to go with Maksym and Dimitri. Escort them to Lviv. They'll need your protection to get through the Rusviet patrols.'

Kirov raised an eyebrow, his lips curling into a grin. 'Us? Babysitting duty?' He gave a mock salute, though there was a hint of genuine respect in his voice. 'All right, Major. But don't expect us to play nice.'

Orlov chuckled, shaking his head. 'We'll get them there in one piece, sir. Just don't be surprised if Kirov complains the whole way.'

Veselov's stern expression softened into the faintest of smiles. 'I'm counting on it,' he said quietly, before nodding towards the rough dirt road barely visible through the trees. 'Follow that road for about ten klicks. You'll hit a river, and there's an old bridge – cross it at night to avoid drones. Once you're on the other side, head east until you reach the outskirts of Lviv. Kozak's men will find you before you find them.'

Turning back to Maksym, Veselov's expression darkened again, his voice dropping to a more sombre tone. 'This might be our last stand. But if anyone can make it, it's you and your crew. And Sova.' He glanced briefly at Dimitri, who stood by, silent but resolute.

Maksym met the Major's eyes, understanding the gravity of the mission. 'We'll get there,' he promised, voice unwavering, before turning to gather his team.

As they moved towards the path, Kirov clapped Dimitri on the back, nearly knocking him off balance. 'Looks like you're stuck with us, kid,' he said with a smirk. 'But don't worry – we might even teach you a thing or two.'

Dimitri managed a small smile, but before they could continue, a low, rumbling sound filled the air. Dimitri's heart skipped a beat. He turned towards Sova. The lights within her chest had begun to glow again, a sign that she was waking from Deep Sleep. Her systems hummed to life, the low thrum of her core reactor growing stronger with each passing second. Slowly, her head lifted, and her glowing optics flickered, scanning the area as she powered up.

'Sova's awake,' Maksym muttered, relieved. 'That'll help.'

As Sova completed her reboot, the sound of heavy footsteps caught their attention. Katya emerged from the front line, her armoured frame gleaming under the dim light. She had been reinforcing the defences, but now her focus was back on Dimitri and Sova.

'Looks like I'm not too late,' Katya remarked, amused. She scanned Sova with her sensors. 'Fully operational – well, operational enough,' she added with a note of dry humour.

Sova's optics flickered again as she turned her battered frame towards Dimitri. 'Dimitri,' she said softly, her voice carrying a warmth unusual for a machine. 'I'm still here. A bit stiff, maybe, but nothing I can't handle.'

Dimitri exhaled. He stepped closer, his hand instinctively brushing against the cool metal of her frame. 'I thought … I thought I lost you,' he admitted.

'You didn't,' Sova replied, her tone steady and reassuring. 'It'll take more than a collapsed bridge to stop me. Besides, I couldn't leave you to handle all this alone.'

A relieved smile crept across Dimitri's face. 'You scared me,' he murmured.

'I'm sorry,' Sova said, a faint echo of emotion laced in her words. 'But I'm here now. And we still have work to do.'

Katya stepped forward, interrupting the moment. 'Touching as this is, we don't have time to stand around reminiscing. Lviv isn't going to defend itself.'

Dimitri nodded, his bond with Sova renewed. Together, the group – Dimitri, Maksym, Katya, and the two Sentinels – readied themselves. The Sentinels flanked them, their weapons poised, as they began their trek towards Lviv.

Chapter 12 – Lviv

The afternoon sun filtered through the forest canopy, casting shifting patches of light onto the group as they trudged through the underbrush. Dimitri felt a strange sense of security within Sova's cockpit. He monitored the surroundings through Sova's sensors, alert for any sign of movement.

Dimitri leaned forward in the cockpit, his voice soft. 'Sova, are you feeling better now?'

'The damage was extensive,' she replied, quietly, warmly. 'But the repairs are sufficient. I am … operational again, Dimitri. Thank you for your concern.'

A small smile flickered across his face as he rested a hand on the console. 'You scared me back there. I thought we were going to lose you.'

'I am designed to endure. But your worry … is noted. It is a rare and valuable trait.'

A burst of static crackled in his headset, followed by Maksym's familiar voice, heavy with mock seriousness. 'Don't let her fool you, kid. Machines don't feel emotions – unless you count being perpetually annoyed at their pilots.'

Dimitri chuckled, shaking his head. 'Pretty sure she's more patient than you.'

'Affirmative,' Sova interjected with amusement. 'My patience reserves are significantly higher than Maksym's.'

'All right, all right, team up on the human, why don't you?' Maksym snorted. 'Just remember, Sova, if I didn't patch you up, you'd still be face down in a ravine.'

'Correction,' Sova said evenly. 'Katya extracted me from the ravine. Your assistance was limited to ensuring Dimitri survived.'

Dimitri laughed. 'She's not wrong, Maksym.'

There was a moment of silence, followed by a good-natured chuckle from Maksym. 'Fine, I'll take the win. But next time we face off against a T90 … hold up.' His voice dropped abruptly to a whisper. 'We've got company.'

Ahead, barely visible through the trees, were three Velociraptors – moving in unison. Their heads swivelled, scanning the area for potential threats.

'Velociraptor scouting party,' Maksym muttered. 'If they spot us, we'll be in trouble.'

Dimitri's voice came quietly through the comms, edged with nerves. 'How did a scouting party make it behind the Ukrainian front line?'

Maksym didn't answer immediately, eyes fixed on the Velociraptors. 'No idea,' he finally whispered. 'But if they've made it this far, we're either compromised, or they've found a gap we don't know about.'

'We should take them out now,' Orlov suggested into his comms, gripping his Longbow.

'No,' Maksym replied, a plan forming in his mind. 'We need information. If we can capture one of them alive, we might learn something about their plans.'

Dimitri felt his pulse quicken. 'How do we do that?' he asked.

'Sova can disable one,' Maksym said, 'but you need to hit it with non-lethal force. Aim for the legs; take out its mobility.'

'I've got a better idea,' Sova responded.

The group crept forward, taking cover behind the trees, and Sova positioned herself for an attack. Dimitri's nerves tingled. 'Ready when you are,' he murmured.

'Now!' Maksym ordered.

Sova surged forward, bursting through the foliage. The Velociraptors spun around, sensors flaring as they detected the sudden movement, but it was too late. Sova's left arm shot out, her reinforced hand clamping around the leg of the nearest machine. With a swift movement, she yanked hard, sending the Velociraptor crashing to the ground.

The machine screeched, its servos whining in protest as its limbs flailed wildly. A burst of erratic gunfire erupted from its mounted miniguns, shredding through nearby trees and cutting jagged lines across the forest floor.

'Disable it!' Maksym shouted, and Dimitri responded with a flick of his foot on the controls, directing Sova to

212

stomp down on the Velociraptor's thighs, while at the same time both her arms yanked the arms from the torso, disabling the miniguns. The machine thrashed, trying to twist free, but Sova's heavy foot was unyielding.

The other two Velociraptors opened fire, their weapons spitting bullets that ricocheted harmlessly off Sova's armour. Kirov and Orlov moved swiftly, flanking the attackers and opening fire, their high explosive shots precise and deadly. Within seconds, the two remaining Velociraptors lay motionless, their limbs twitching as sparks flickered across their bodies.

Inside the cockpit, Dimitri watched the struggling machine underfoot as it finally went still, the red glow of its eyes flickering as if in defiance. 'We've got it,' he said, exhaling a breath he hadn't realized he'd been holding.

Maksym approached the downed Velociraptor, his expression hard. 'Let's see what secrets you're hiding,' he muttered, pulling out a small data probe. He knelt next to the machine's head and inserted the probe into a port at its base.

From the treeline, Kirov spoke up, his deep voice laced with dry amusement. 'I'd wager not much. Looks like we've already disarmed it.'

Orlov chimed in, his tone lighter, almost cheerful. 'Disarmed? You mean dismantled. I don't think it could even applaud our performance.'

Maksym snorted without looking up. 'You two done yet? Some of us are trying to work here.'

'Just trying to lighten the mood,' Kirov replied with mock innocence.

Katya's voice cut in, smooth and sharp. 'If you're all done with your stand-up routine, perhaps one of you would like to keep an eye out for reinforcements while Maksym digs for treasure.'

Maksym smirked as he continued working. 'She's got a point. Maybe keep those sensors scanning instead of cracking jokes.'

Kirov let out a low hum, pretending to be offended. 'Fine. But if more Velociraptors come hunting, don't say we didn't keep things interesting.'

Dimitri cracked a grin, shaking his head as he watched the exchange.

As they pressed westward, the landscape shifted from dense forests to scattered, war-torn villages, each a shadow of what once was. The remnants of small communities clung to the edge of the road, half-destroyed buildings leaning precariously, their walls scarred by artillery fire and their roofs caved in. Fields that once stretched green and fertile were now overgrown, pockmarked by craters or charred from the fires of war.

Dimitri peered through Sova's cockpit, eyes wide as they marched through the dilapidated settlements. Small houses with broken windows and patchwork roofs revealed the hardships endured by the villagers. A few men, makeshift weapons in hand, stood guard, their eyes sharp but hollow, ready to defend their last remnants of home.

As Katya and Sova trudged through the villages, people gazed up at them with a mixture of fear and awe, whispering among themselves. Others watched in silence, expressions unreadable, knowing too well the devastation that machines like these could bring.

Finally, the group moved past the last of the villages and the city of Lviv loomed on the horizon, the atmosphere grew heavier.

From Katya's cockpit, Maksym took in the scene. The sight of Lviv stirred something deep within him. This was *his* city, a place where memories of a life before the war lingered. But more than that, it stood as a symbol of defiance, holding out against all odds, resisting the relentless advance of the Rusviet forces. His jaw tightened as he scanned the horizon, emotions swirling within him. The ruins were heartbreaking, yet the city still stood, scarred but unbroken, a beacon of resistance in a world on the brink of collapse.

Maksym leaned forward in Katya's cramped cockpit, the glow of her instruments casting his face in pale light. He toggled the comms. 'We made it,' he whispered, voice tight with emotion. 'Lviv … still standing.'

Dimitri's voice crackled through the shared frequency. 'It's beautiful,' he murmured.

Maksym refocused, flipping the comms to an encrypted frequency. 'Command, this is Falcon Bravo Two Zero. I'm inbound with a high-value asset and support units. Requesting access codes and permission to enter the eastern perimeter. Do you copy?'

Silence stretched before them, filled only by the faint hum of Katya's systems and the rhythmic clinking of her footsteps as she moved. Then static, followed by a sharp voice, cut through. 'Identify your units, Falcon Bravo Two Zero. One of your "assets" is reading as Rusviet hardware. Explain.'

Maksym clenched his jaw. 'Katya is an ex-Rusviet T90 UX, reprogrammed and under my command. She's part

216

of the Resistance now. Verify my ID and listen carefully –
we're carrying critical intelligence and reinforcements.
We need entry. Immediately.'

Another pause, this one heavier, as if the operator wasn't
sure whether to believe him. Then the voice returned,
slightly more measured. 'Verification required. Hold your
position while we confirm your credentials. Any
deviation and that T90 will be treated as hostile.'

'Understood,' Maksym replied, maintaining a calm tone.
He switched to the internal frequency. 'Katya, keep your
posture low. No sudden moves. They're jumpy.'

'Of course,' Katya replied, her voice smooth and
unwavering. 'I would prefer not to be obliterated by
friendly fire.'

Dimitri chimed in nervously. 'Are they going to let us
in?'

'They will,' Maksym said, though his grip on the controls
betrayed his tension.

The comms crackled again. 'Verification complete.
Sending access codes now.' A series of tones followed,
and a string of numbers appeared on Katya's display.
'Proceed to Gate Five then Command Central sector 2B,

and welcome home Maksym. And keep that T90 on a short leash.'

'Copy that. Maksym out.' He exhaled and glanced at Katya's interior displays. 'Let's move. Keep it steady and stay close.'

As they approached the towering gates of Lviv, the defences bristled with activity. Soldiers manned fortified positions, their eyes trained on Katya with suspicion, while others whispered and pointed at the unusual sight of a Rusviet war machine walking alongside its enemies. The cobblestone streets were choked with debris – abandoned vehicles, craters from mortar shells, and smoke rising from scattered pockets of burning wreckage. Despite the destruction, remnants of Lviv's grandeur remained. Ornate facades and domed churches stood cracked and pockmarked, but still they stood.

They entered the eastern district, where whole blocks had been flattened, leaving only the hollowed-out shells of buildings. Dimitri's eyes lingered on a once-majestic opera house, now buried under rubble, its pillars cracked but standing defiantly.

Amidst the destruction, life clung on. Civilians moved through the streets with purpose, faces haggard but determined. Soldiers dug trenches and reinforced barricades with whatever they could find. Maksym observed them with quiet respect as they passed.

The arrival of the group caused a stir. Eyes widened in awe and fear as Sova's and Katya's towering forms strode through the streets. Civilians tending to the wounded froze, staring up at the hulking machines. Mothers pulled their children close. Soldiers straightened, their fatigued expressions giving way to something between disbelief and hope.

'Look! It's one of ours … is it?' someone muttered.

'Are they friendly?' another asked, eyeing Katya warily.

Whispers spread through the crowd, curiosity and fear in their voices. The Sentinels followed, their footfalls echoing through the streets. Some soldiers saluted, recognizing the significance of their arrival, while others simply stared, mouths agape.

As they pressed deeper into the city, the streets narrowed. The distant rumble of artillery fire echoed in the background, while the command centre loomed ahead – a squat, reinforced structure behind layers of barricades and sandbags. Soldiers moved around the perimeter, preparing for what was likely the final stand.

Maksym led the group towards the entrance, his eyes scanning the area. He nodded to the guards at the gate, who stepped aside, recognizing the importance of the moment.

'Command is just through here,' Maksym muttered to Dimitri.

Inside the dimly lit command centre, General Kozak stood tall at the head of the map table. His weathered face, marked with deep lines, remained expressionless as his eyes scanned the maps before him. Dusty lamps cast shadows over the table, where red-inked lines sketched out the advancing Rusviet forces. His uniform, though tidy, bore the stains of war: a ripped seam on his sleeve, frayed edges on his collar.

General Kozak gestured for Maksym to step forward. 'You've done well,' he began, offering a brief nod to Dimitri. 'The data you extracted from the T-90VX – or should I say 'Kayta' – on the train has given us invaluable insight. We've been able to confirm their troop movements, supply lines, and even parts of their command structure. It's clear now: the Rusviets have been using an underground network across Ukraine and Poland to support their war machines.'

He tapped the map, and a holographic projection flickered to life. 'What's more, intel from the Steel Works confirms they intend to initiate a major assault using a Signals Drone stationed at the castle ruins outside Lviv. This drone will broadcast orders to their entire army of T90 Volkovs at dawn, directing them into our defences. We also know from that hapless Velociraptor Scout you interrogated inside our lines that all other forces will hold back from the first T90 assault wave.'

Kozak's gaze sharpened. 'But we have an opportunity. Instead of destroying the drone, you're going to infiltrate the castle tonight, just before midnight. Your mission is to reprogram the drone to broadcast a new set of orders: instructing every T90 Volkov in the region to enter their Deep Sleep mode.'

The officers exchanged looks. Kozak continued, 'By sending them into Deep Sleep, we'll neutralize the vast bulk of Rusviet war machines, allowing us to launch a surprise counterassault when they're most vulnerable.'

Maksym nodded, absorbing the information. 'What's our insertion plan?' he asked.

'We'll drop you in at high altitude,' Kozak replied, pointing to a spot on the map close to the castle's perimeter. 'You, Dimitri, Sova and the two Sentinels will glide in on specially constructed 3D printed wingsuits at 0300 hours. Once inside, secure the Signals Drone and upload the reprogramming data. But you must be quick. Once the new orders are transmitted, we'll only have a small window before they realise something's wrong. Katya will hold a separate position near the Castle, as backup if necessary.'

Dimitri shifted, listening intently. 'And the T90s, will they stay asleep?' he asked.

'The moment they enter Deep Sleep mode, they'll be rendered inactive,' Kozak explained. 'We'll have a brief period to strike while they're vulnerable, and that's when we launch our full assault.'

Kozak glanced around the room before turning back to Maksym and Dimitri. 'This mission is our best chance to shift the tide in our favour. If you succeed, we'll cripple the vast bulk of their army.'

Maksym tightened his jaw. 'We'll get it done,' he promised.

General Kozak's gaze lingered on Dimitri for a moment before he continued. 'There's something else you need to know,' he began. 'There was serious discussion among the high command about swapping you out, Dimitri, for a more experienced pilot for this mission.'

Dimitri felt his stomach drop, a chill running through him. He knew he wasn't the most skilled pilot, but the thought of being replaced still stung.

Kozak continued, his voice softening. 'You see, this mission is unlike anything we've faced before. It requires precision, quick thinking, and the ability to adapt under extreme pressure. Naturally, the commanders were concerned about sending someone as young as you – someone without years of combat experience – into the heart of enemy territory.'

He paused, letting his words sink in. 'But Sova ... she's chosen you. The bond you've formed, the way you've already led her into battle and accomplished what more seasoned pilots couldn't – it's something they can't ignore. We've never seen a War Machine bond this deeply with a pilot before, and quite frankly, it's your connection with Sova that has given us every advantage we've managed to seize so far.'

The General stepped closer, his eyes locked on Dimitri's. 'In the end, I made the decision to allow you on this mission, if you choose to accept it. Not because you're the most experienced, but because you've proven that you and Sova are a team. And in this war, that bond might just be the one thing that turns the tide.'

Dimitri swallowed hard. 'I accept,' he said, voice steady despite the nerves gnawing at him. 'I won't let you down, sir.'

Kozak nodded, a hint of respect flashing in his eyes. 'Then prepare yourself, Pilot Dimitri. We're counting on you to be our sword and shield.'

As the group turned to leave, Kozak's voice softened. 'Dimitri,' he called, 'this isn't just about Lviv. Sova found something else hidden within Katya's data, something she didn't tell you at the time – your family. They're alive, working in a labour camp east of the front lines.'

Dimitri froze. 'My parents?'

Kozak nodded. 'Yes. Complete this mission, and we'll have the leverage we need to rescue them.'

Dimitri straightened, feeling the full weight of the responsibility on his shoulders. 'We won't fail,' he vowed.

General Kozak's voice took on a commanding tone again. 'Then get moving. Lviv is counting on you.'

Chapter 13 – Castle

Hours later, Dimitri sat inside Sova's dimly lit cockpit, his heart hammering in his chest. The wind howled outside the aircraft's cargo hold as they soared high above the darkened landscape. His black thermal suit clung to him, masking his heat signature, but it did little to stop sweat forming on his palms. His hands gripped the controls, knuckles white, eyes darting across the interface in front of him, which showed their current flight path towards the castle.

The plan was straightforward yet daunting: Sova would power down almost entirely during the descent, reducing her heat signature to avoid detection by the Rusviet's sensors. This meant that, for the duration of the drop, all critical systems would be offline, leaving Dimitri with the sole responsibility of maintaining balance and control of Sova and her wingsuit.

Beside him, Maksym adjusted his wingsuit, calm and methodical as ever. 'You ready?' he asked, looking up at Sova's cockpit, voice steady despite the turbulence around them.

Dimitri nodded, swallowing hard. 'As ready as I'll ever be.'

Maksym glanced at the wings folded against Sova's back, sleek and reinforced. 'You know,' he said with a smirk, 'they tell me this 3D printed wingsuit was tested once before on an AWMa.'

Dimitri arched an eyebrow. 'And did it work?'

Maksym's grin widened. 'Depends on your definition of 'worked.' They say it glided perfectly … right before it crashed into a mountain.'

Sova's voice cut in, smooth and unbothered. 'I assure you, Dimitri, this time will be different.'

'Well, that's comforting,' Dimitri muttered, tightening his grip on the controls. 'Let's hope we stick the landing.'

'Remember the plan,' Maksym reminded him. 'You control the descent until 3,000 feet. Then we power her on.'

Suddenly, a gruff voice crackled over the comms. 'You two about done with your pep talk?' It was Kirov, perched on the edge of the cargo hold with Orlov, both Sentinels prepping for the drop. 'Some of us have real work to do.'

Orlov smirked, elbowing his partner. 'Careful, Kirov. You might hurt their feelings. Besides, you're just mad you don't get to ride in the fancy War Machine.'

'Fancy? Please,' Kirov grunted. 'I've seen cargo crates with more personality. I'd rather trust my own two legs than rely on that hunk of metal.'

'You two finished?' Maksym cut in, an exasperated edge to his voice. 'We've got a mission to complete.'

Kirov gave a mock salute. 'Just keeping things light, Captain.'

Dimitri couldn't help but smile, the brief exchange easing some of the tension in his chest. 'You ready, Sova?' he asked quietly.

'Ready when you are, Pilot Dimitri,' Sova replied.

Suddenly, a mechanical hum filled the cabin and a loader bot rolled towards the open ramp. Its yellow optics gleamed mischievously as its arms extended towards Sova's frame. 'Ah, Sova! Good to see you again, my old friend,' the bot said in a thick Ukrainian accent, its synthesized voice full of mock cheer. 'Off for another little tumble, are we?'

Sova's voice, calm but irritated, chimed through Dimitri's earpiece. 'Enough, Bohdan. I'd appreciate it if you skipped the commentary and just did your job.'

Bohdan let out a laugh as he worked to secure Sova to the drop mechanism. 'Ah, Sova, you wound me! Where's your sense of humour? You know, before every drop I like to tell a little joke.'

Dimitri, despite his nerves, couldn't help but glance at the loader bot. 'A joke?'

Bohdan swivelled to look up at the cockpit, his glowing optics narrowing conspiratorially. 'What's the last thing that goes through an AWMa's mind as it falls from 30,000 feet?'

Dimitri blinked, taken aback. 'I don't know. What?'

'Her feet.'

There was a beat of silence before Bohdan burst into a fit of laughter. 'Get it? 'Cause you're gonna hit the ground and your feet will go through—'

'Bohdan,' Sova interrupted, 'we're not going to hit the ground headfirst. Now release us before I make sure you never tell another joke again.'

The loader let out a theatrical sigh. 'Fine, fine. You know, Sova, your lack of appreciation for comedy is tragic.' He turned to Maksym. 'Your team ready for rapid descent?' Maksym nodded, adjusting his wingsuit while he spoke. 'Power down, Sova. Activate only when your sensors indicate we're at 3,000 feet.'
'Powering down now,' Sova responded cooly.

Dimitri held his breath. Just days ago, he was sitting on his hill, listening to the sounds of war. Now he was trying to change the course of it. The plane rumbled and bounced in the turbulence, adding to his anxiety. His hands gripped the cockpit seat, leg shaking with nerves. The release mechanism activated, and he felt himself tipping forward into a fast plummet, the dark world below rushing up at them.

For a terrifying second, the cockpit went weightless. The wind howled as they plummeted, the ground approaching with dizzying speed. Dimitri's hands gripped the controls, frantically adjusting their descent, just as he'd practiced hours earlier in the simulator. Sova's wings, though motionless, extended slightly, helping steady the fall.

'Keep her level,' Maksym's voice came through the comms. 'You're doing fine. Just keep it steady.' Dimitri glanced sideways through Sova's cockpit, the dim light of the moon barely illuminating the world around them. To his right, he could make out the dark, sleek forms of Maksym and the two Sentinels slicing through the air, moving in perfect synchrony.

Maksym led the way, his arms and legs pinned straight back. The Sentinels flanked him on either side, their bodies flying like arrows in the darkness, wingsuits giving them the ability to glide at incredible speed. Their Longbow rifles and miniguns were slung across their fronts, ready for action below.

The wind screamed outside the cockpit as Dimitri's shaking hands continued to work the interface, keeping Sova from tumbling or spinning wildly.

'Almost there ... now!' Maksym shouted through the comms.

Dimitri's hand flew to the switch, flipping it with a surge of panic and adrenaline. For a heartbeat, nothing happened. The cockpit was silent, save for the howl of the wind rushing past. Then Sova's systems roared to life, lights flickering on as her systems reactivated. Control panels lit up, and Dimitri felt the familiar, steady presence of Sova envelop him once more.

'I've got it, Dimitri,' Sova's calm voice purred in his ear, her wings adjusting their angle with precision as they slowed their descent. 'Nice work keeping me in one piece. Let's make this landing smooth.'

With the machine now in full control, Sova stabilised their trajectory. Dimitri let out a long, shaky breath. The earth still rushed towards them, but it was no longer a headlong plunge into darkness.

Beside them, Maksym and the pair of Sentinels glided silently towards the castle ruins in their wingsuits, already stabilising themselves for a smooth landing. Dimitri guided Sova towards the courtyard, his hands trembling less now as they neared their target. Sova's cockpit flared, bringing up targets: Velociraptors on the perimeter – an anti-missile battery in the courtyard – all seemingly unaware of their approach. The castle walls loomed large, ancient and imposing. Three hundred feet. One hundred feet. Dimitri could see the turrets of the old castle, standing before them like guardians.

Sova retracted her wings at the last moment, a low hiss signalling their touchdown as she landed with a heavy thud. Dimitri's legs wobbled as he released the controls, feeling both relief and adrenaline flood his system.

Maksym touched down a few seconds later, glancing at the imposing machine beside him. 'Good landing, kid,' he said, as if this were just another day in the field.

But there was no time to celebrate. The moment their feet hit the ground, the Rusviet's automated defences sprang to life. Patrol Drones began circling, their lights flickering across the perimeter, and Velociraptors charged towards the sound of their arrival.

Kirov and Orlov landed shortly after. Orlov cracked his neck, loosening up. 'Guess we've got some party crashers,' he muttered, drawing his Longbow and minigun.

Kirov smirked. 'About time. I was getting bored up there.'

As they sprinted towards the castle's entrance, the Velociraptors stationed along the castle walls began to fire down on them, their slim, angular frames silhouetted against the dark sky. 'Sentinels, take out those Velociraptors!' Maksym barked, barely pausing to issue the command.

'With pleasure,' Kirov replied, his rifle already snapping up to his shoulder. He squeezed the trigger, and a precise burst of fire took out the nearest Velociraptor, sending it sprawling over the edge of the wall. Orlov followed suit, picking off another with a single shot.

'Try to leave a few for me!' Orlov called out, a grin spreading across his face.

'No promises,' Kirov shot back, his eyes narrowing as he lined up another shot.

Meanwhile, Sova's attention was focused on the swarm of drones that had begun to descend from the sky. 'Incoming SD1 Mini Drones,' she said. 'Engaging now.'

Sova's minigun roared to life, the barrel spinning as it spewed tracer fire into the approaching swarm. The first wave of drones exploded midair, raining debris over the courtyard.

'More are coming!' Dimitri shouted, glancing up to see another wave of drones emerging from behind the castle's ruined towers.

Sova adjusted her aim, the minigun blazing, and tore through the incoming drones with ruthless efficiency. Sparks lit up the sky as drone after drone disintegrated under the onslaught. 'I've got them,' she said, her voice unwavering.

'Kirov, Orlov, keep those Velociraptors off us!' Maksym shouted as he dashed across the open courtyard. Another Velociraptor appeared, training its shoulder-mounted missile on Sova, but before it could fire, Orlov took it down with a well-timed shot.

'Target down,' Orlov said with a hint of satisfaction.

'Nice shot,' Kirov muttered, picking off another Velociraptor with pinpoint accuracy. 'But you're still two behind me.'

'Not that anyone's counting,' Orlov retorted, rolling his eyes.

With the Velociraptors on the castle walls being systematically taken out by the Sentinels, Sova was able to focus entirely on the drones. Dimitri felt a surge of confidence as he watched the Velociraptors crumble under the combined fire of Kirov and Orlov.
'Sova, time for me to join Maksym,' Dimitri shouted, nerves causing his voice to reach breaking point.
Sova crouched low, and the cockpit opened.
'Dimitri, you're good to go, just don't stop for a tea break, okay?' crackled Kirov, as he and Orlov kept picking off targets.

'Roger that, Kirov!' Dimitri called into his comms before clambering out of the cockpit, a short-barrelled automatic machine gun slung over his shoulder, and dropping to the castle cobblestones. He paused for a moment to check for snipers, then ran to the doorway where Maksym was pressed up against the decaying stonework.

Out of the corner of his eye, Maksym noticed something unmistakable: an ominous craft stationed at the far end of the castle grounds. The insignia was a gleaming red star encircled by the black crest of the High Commissariat – the same craft they had seen at the Steel Works. The High Commander was here.

Behind them, Sova unleashed a final barrage, her minigun glowing red-hot as it shredded the remaining drones. Debris clattered around them, and with one last explosion, the courtyard fell silent.

'Castle perimeter secured,' Sova reported, her voice calm as ever. 'Proceed with mission objective.'

The air inside the castle was thick with dust, the cold wind biting at their skin. Dimitri's breath came in visible puffs as they raced through the dark, labyrinthine corridors. Moonlight seeped through cracks in the walls, casting long, eerie shadows across the crumbling stonework.

'Almost there,' Maksym muttered, his voice barely audible over the distant sounds of an erupting gun battle behind them. *More reinforcements to keep Sova and the Sentinels busy,* he thought. He and Dimitri both knew the drones wouldn't stop. Time was running out.

'We should be getting close,' Maksym whispered, glancing back at Dimitri. 'Stay alert. These stairs are a prime spot for an ambush.'

Dimitri nodded, his eyes scanning the upward curve of the stairwell, unsure what dangers lay ahead. His heart raced – not just from the adrenaline but from the struggle to keep pace with Maksym. His limp, though less noticeable now, still tugged at his energy.

Following Maksym, he adjusted his machine gun. He hadn't had much practice with it back at Lviv and hoped he wouldn't have to use it. As they neared the top of the stairs, a deep hum echoed throughout the stone passage.

'Do you hear that?' Dimitri whispered, voice tense.

'Yeah,' Maksym replied, his hand instinctively moving to the grip of his weapon. 'Get ready.'

At the top of the castle stairs, they entered a large, dimly lit hall. Maksym's flashlight beam swept across the stone walls, revealing faded murals of long-forgotten battles. In the centre of the room stood a long banqueting table flanked by worn bench seats. At the far end, an older man, broad-shouldered in a sleek military uniform sat calmly.

'Maksym!' Dimitri whispered, his voice trembling, 'it's the . . .'

'High Commander,' Maksym confirmed in a steely tone, raising his rifle to aim at the figure.

'Oh, don't be so hostile,' the seated man said jovially, leaning back with an air of confidence. 'Come, sit. You're too late to stop our plans anyway – the signals drone is moments away from downloading its final instructions. And this castle is the perfect place to watch the final destruction of what's left of your country.'

As if to punctuate his words, a crimson glint flickered from the shadows near the Commander's shoulder. Stepping into the dim light, the menacing black frame of his bodyguard emerged – the S10 Velociraptor from the Steel Works. Twin miniguns locked onto Maksym and Dimitri, the machine's glowing optics unblinking as it sized them up.

'What's stopping me from shooting you right now, Commander?' Maksym shouted, his finger poised on the trigger, his body tense and ready.

'You could, I suppose,' the Commander mused, unfazed. 'Our intel tells me it was your team that caused us so much trouble these past few days.' He leaned back, hand resting under his chin as if considering the idea. 'But before you do, remember – both you and the boy beside you would be dead in seconds.' He gestured towards his silent Bodyguard, its guns still trained on them. 'We could use someone like you. Your friends outside could join us, help expand the Empire. Why fight when you could help us?'

'I'm not his son, and you'll never succeed!' Dimitri yelled, rage overtaking his fear as he raised his rifle, aiming at the Guardian.

'Don't say a word,' Maksym hissed, stepping protectively in front of Dimitri, shielding him from the machine's gaze.

The Commander's smile widened. 'Ah, so the pieces fall into place. You're Dimitri, the boy from the orphanage – the one who escaped with the AWMa that stands just outside.' His voice softened, almost gentle. 'Dimitri, we have your parents. They're alive, being held at a camp just east of Moscow. I can reunite you. Tell your friend to stand down, and I'll personally make you a family again.'

Dimitri's heart leapt at the mention of his parents. His breath caught, eyes widening with hope. 'I … I … '

'I would rather save my country,' he stammered, tears streaking his face.

The Commander sighed. 'Pity. I thought I was being rather generous. Fenrir, shoot our gue-'

A loud clanking echoed through the hall. 'Hey folks, what's for dinner?' came a casual voice from the doorway.

Kirov sauntered in, unslinging his Longbow rifle with a casual smirk. He surveyed the scene, his eyes locking on the Guardian. 'Ah, a Velociraptor for starters,' he quipped, raising his Longbow.

Fenrir shifted, one minigun whirring towards Kirov while the other stayed locked on Maksym and Dimitri. But Kirov was faster. Before anyone could react, he fired. The explosive round struck the barrel of the Velociraptor's gun aimed at Dimitri, sending a shower of sparks as the metal buckled and twisted. The weapon faltered, its barrel bent and useless.

Immediately, Fenrir returned fire with the remaining minigun, but the rounds ricocheted harmlessly off Kirov's armour. Maksym didn't hesitate – he grabbed Dimitri, pulling him under the table as gunfire peppered the air above them.

The Commander's voice cut through the chaos, his laughter cold and menacing. 'Fenrir doesn't need a gun to handle my enemies.' At his signal, Fenrir leaped onto the table, its arms outstretched, inviting Kirov into hand-to-hand combat.

The moment Fenrir sprang from the table, Kirov sprinted forward, tossing aside his Longbow. The Velociraptor moved with deadly speed, its black frame a blur as it closed in on Maksym and Dimitri beneath the table. Just as its massive arms came crashing down, Kirov intercepted, diving shoulder-first into Fenrir's side, knocking it off course.

They tumbled across the stone floor, and Kirov quickly regained his footing, delivering a hard punch to Fenrir's chest. Sparks flew as his fist connected with the armoured plating, but Fenrir barely flinched. With inhuman speed, it retaliated, its fist slamming into Kirov's side and launching him into the wall.

Kirov staggered to his feet, his systems strained but operational, just as Fenrir charged again. Before they could collide, a sharp metallic snap cut through the air – Razorcoil. In an instant, the whip-like weapon, mounted on Fenrir's left arm, lashed out in a blur. The high-tensile coil wrapped around Kirov's torso, its metal tendrils tightening viciously.

Kirov barely had time to react before a sudden electrical charge surged through the coil, crackling with energy. The shockwave hit him like a hammer, sending him flying backwards. His body slammed into the stone wall with a deafening thud, cracks spidering through the ancient masonry as dust and debris rained down.

Dazed, Kirov struggled to recover, his servos groaning in protest as his systems fought to regain stability. Fenrir advanced, the Razorcoil retracting back into its arm, preparing for the next strike. Fenrir's red sensors locked onto Kirov, its intent unmistakable. Kirov, still dazed and pinned against the stone wall from the Razorcoil's brutal discharge, struggled to move as Fenrir advanced. Without hesitation, the bodyguard lunged, its powerful arms locking around Kirov's torso with a crushing grip.

Maksym, still tucked beneath the table, fired several rounds at Fenrir, but the bullets ricocheted harmlessly off its thick armour. Desperate, he lunged forward, trying to pry the machine off Kirov, but it was like trying to move a mountain. Fenrir barely registered his efforts, its focus entirely on Kirov as it tightened its hold.

Kirov's laboured, machine-like gasps echoed in the room as his strength began to falter against Fenrir's relentless onslaught. The servos inside the war machine whirred, preparing for a final, devastating blow that would crush the life from him.

Suddenly, Orlov burst into the room, assessing the scene in an instant. 'Kirov, roll left! One meter!' he screamed.

Kirov reacted immediately, wrenching his body to the left just as Orlov slammed into both him and Fenrir with full force. The collision sent all three crashing through the crumbling stone wall. The ancient masonry gave way with a deafening crack, and they plummeted towards the courtyard below.

They hit the ground hard, dust and rubble billowing up from the collapse, clouding the air. Kirov struggled to his knees, barely able to move, his systems strained. Fenrir, unrelenting, was already rising, its glowing red sensors locked onto Kirov, ready to finish the job.

But before Fenrir could strike, a massive shadow loomed over them.

It was Sova.

Maksym stood up and glanced towards the end of the long table where the Commander had been seated. The chair was empty, the Commander already disappearing at the far end of the great hall.

'We must move, Dimitri – it could already be too late,' Maksym said, muttering the last part half to himself. His eyes caught the doorway leading to another staircase. From the maps, he knew this was the way to the top of the tower.

Dimitri and Maksym sprinted towards the base of the final staircase, where the ancient stone steps spiralled upward into darkness. They exchanged a brief glance – there was no time to waste. Their footsteps echoed on the cold, uneven stone as they rushed the stairwell.

At the top, a heavy wooden door blocked their path. It was worn but solid, reinforced with iron bands that glinted faintly. Maksym reached for a small explosive charge from his gear, quickly planting it at the door's centre.

'Stand back,' Maksym whispered, his voice calm but urgent. In seconds, a muted *thud* reverberated through the air, followed by the splintering sound of wood as the door blew inward.

Maksym moved first, entering the tower's inner chamber. It was dark, with crumbling stone walls surrounding a central platform where the Rusviet Signal Drone hovered. The low hum of its systems filled the room, glowing softly.

At the far end of the chamber, a humanoid AI robot technician hunched over a control terminal, its metallic fingers moving quickly. The faint hum of servos accompanied its motions as it adjusted commands on the screen, completely oblivious to Maksym and Dimitri. Its glowing red eyes focused solely on the task at hand – programming new orders for the Signal Drone to relay to the Rusviet war machines.

'Go!' Dimitri shouted, taking command, his voice sharp.

Maksym launched into action, sprinting towards the technician. The robot's sensors flickered in recognition, but it was too late to defend itself. Maksym's combat-honed instincts kicked in as he drove forward, his movements swift and precise.

The AI technician turned, its head swivelling unnaturally fast to face him, but Maksym was faster. With a powerful strike, he smashed the robot's control panel chest, sending it crashing into the stone floor. A jarring metallic clatter echoed through the chamber as the technician's limbs twitched and sparked from the impact. Its eyes flickered erratically before going dark.

Meanwhile, Dimitri's focus was on the drone. It scanned its surroundings, unaware of the danger. Dimitri charged forward, lunging towards the drone as it powered up, anticipating its chance to relay critical orders to the vast army of T90s. His hands gripped the cool metal chassis, using every ounce of strength to wrestle the machine down, locking it into place. The drone buzzed violently, but Dimitri held firm.

'Maksym!' Dimitri yelled over the sound of the drone's thrumming energy. Maksym rushed to the terminal. Whipping out the device from the Ukrainian tech team, he jammed it into the port, his fingers moving furiously as he initiated the reprogramming command. Sweat dripped down his forehead, but his expression was focused.

The seconds stretched into what seemed like minutes. Dimitri could feel the drone straining against his grip, its systems fighting back as it tried to execute its orders. His muscles burned, but he refused to let go.

Finally, the terminal emitted a sharp beep. Maksym's eyes lit up in triumph. 'Got it!' he shouted. His fingers flew over the keys, and with a final press, the virus uploaded. Dimitri watched as the drone's lights flickered briefly, then stabilised, dimming.

'It's done,' Maksym confirmed, his voice filled with a mixture of relief and exhilaration. 'The orders are changed. The Rusviet war machines will now go into hibernation mode.'

Dimitri released the drone, stepping back as its systems powered down. For a moment, silence filled the chamber, save for their ragged breaths.

As Dimitri and Maksym made their way back down the spiralling stairs, the sounds of battle had faded into eerie silence. The air was thick with the scent of smoke and scorched metal. When they reached the courtyard, they found Sova standing tall amidst the carnage. The Guardian lay in pieces, limbs torn, the Razorcoil resting limply on the ground.

Sova,' Dimitri whispered, feeling both relief and awe as they approached her.

'All threats neutralised,' Sova's calm voice echoed through the courtyard, her glowing eyes scanning for any remaining danger.

Nearby, the two Sentinels were still on alert, their heads swivelling back and forth, methodically scanning the area.

'Threat level: zero,' one of them remarked dryly.

The second Sentinel glanced at him. 'We'll keep scanning anyway. You know, just in case a shrub looks at us funny.'

Above them, the Signals Drone hovered, its red light blinking steadily but without movement.

Chapter 14 – Signal

The Signals Drone hovered obediently above the old stone castle, its silent thrumming a stark contrast to the tension building on the ground below. Maksym and Dimitri stood side by side, their eyes fixed on the hovering machine. The cool evening wind swept across the castle's battlements, stirring the quiet that now surrounded them.

'Maksym,' Sova said, 'what exact steps did you take to reprogram the Signals Drone?'

Maksym crossed his arms, staring up at the drone. 'Well, I rerouted the signal commands, then tweaked its targeting parameters to relay the order to all T90s to enter Deep Sleep. I adjusted the frequency – narrowband to wideband – then set the pulse intervals to …' He trailed off, his eyes narrowing as if recalling the final step.

Sova's tone remained patient, though her words carried weight. 'What was the final step, Maksym?'

Maksym scratched his head, a knot tightening in his stomach. 'Well, I … I hit all the keys, right?' His gaze shifted to Dimitri, who was staring at him with growing concern.

'Maksym,' Sova pressed, 'did you press 'Enter' to confirm the command?'

Maksym blinked, his mouth opening slightly in realization. 'Enter … oh, no.'

Dimitri's eyes shot to the horizon. A distant hum, growing louder with each passing second, filled the air. Three Sui-77s Red Vipers – emerged from the dark sky, growing larger as they streaked towards the castle.

'They're coming!' Dimitri shouted. 'Sova let me into your cockpit'.

Maksym swore under his breath, bolting back towards the castle's control room. 'I'll fix the command! Keep them off that drone!'

Sova crouched low to let Dimitri into the cockpit, then stood up, the ground trembling under her weight. Dimitri locked his hands around the control grips of the M-60 Auto Cannon. His heart pounded in his chest, memories of the river battle flooding back – where he had failed to hit his target – panic rising in his chest.

Sova's targeting systems flared to life as she locked onto the incoming Red Vipers. Two of the drones veered out of formation, circling wide to try and flank her. Sova didn't hesitate – her shoulder-mounted missile launcher fired off a round, streaking towards the nearest drone. The first missile connected, blowing the Sui 77 into a ball of flame that dissipated in the evening sky.

The second drone swooped low, twisting and banking as Sova tracked it. She fired again. The missile screamed towards her target – another direct hit – sending the second drone crashing into the ground below with a deafening explosion.

But the third Red Viper was faster, more aggressive, and it broke from its spiralling path to make a beeline for the Signals Drone.

Dimitri's hands shook as he tracked the third drone, his finger hovering over the trigger. 'Steady,' he whispered to himself, heart pounding.

'Focus, Dimitri,' Sova encouraged. 'This time, you won't miss.'

The Red Viper dipped, dodging as it raced closer to the Signals Drone. Dimitri's sights followed it, the world narrowing to the crosshairs of the 20mm Auto Cannon. The pressure built – his breathing, shallow.

The drone came into range. Dimitri squeezed the trigger.

The cannon roared, sending a burst of shells streaking across the sky. For a moment, everything slowed. The shells connected – direct hits – tearing through the Red Vipers frame. The drone spun out of control, its engine sputtering before exploding in mid-air, a fiery ball of debris that rained down harmlessly away from the castle.

Dimitri let out a breath he hadn't realized he'd been holding. His hands still gripped the cannon tightly, but a grin crept across his face.

'Well done, Dimitri,' Sova said, her voice warm with approval. 'The Signals Drone is safe for now.'

Maksym returned from his sprint up the castle steps, giving a quick nod of approval at Dimitri, high up in the cockpit. 'Good work,' he muttered, his gaze sharp as he reached for his comms instead of climbing aboard Sova. Pressing the device to his ear, he opened a direct line to Katya, who was stationed outside the castle ruins, ready as backup.

'Katya, we're in position. Get ready to move on my signal,' Maksym said.

Sova burst through the castle walls with a deafening roar, stone and debris flying in all directions as her massive frame emerged from the ruins. The ground trembled with each step as she moved across the open terrain. Maksym, still on foot, sprinted forward, his eyes darting across the horizon in search of Katya. The Sentinels followed close behind, their weapons scanning for any signs of trouble.

In the distance, Katya's hulking form came into view, moving swiftly towards them from her backup position, her imposing silhouette cutting through the haze of dust and rubble.

As the group left the castle ruins, the midnight sky stretched endlessly before them. The drone hovered briefly at the top of the tower, then, with a faint whirring sound, it glided off, only faint red pulses from its core giving away its location.

From Sova's cockpit, Dimitri watched quietly as the Signals drone slipped away, becoming a mere speck against the night. 'Do you think it'll work?' he whispered into his comms.

Maksym, now in Katya's cockpit, replied gently, 'It's already working.'

Stretched out in front of them Rusviet's front lines were a blaze of activity – the giant war machines moving in tight formations towards Lviv, began to slow.

Dimitri leaned forward, heart pounding. 'Is this … happening?'

Maksym nodded, a grim smile spreading across his face. 'The reprogramming is working. It's shutting them down.'

A ripple of stillness spread across the horizon as the giant war machines ground to a complete halt. Soldiers on both sides watched in stunned silence as their towering metal giants stood frozen, unmoving, like statues caught mid-battle facing Lviv. The front lines, once filled with the roar of gunfire and the clash of machines, now fell eerily silent.

From their cockpits, Dimitri and Maksym could see the Ukrainian defenders stir, eyes wide with realisation. Then, almost as if in unison, the defenders surged forward, tiny figures coming out of the trenches in front of their embattled city. Shouting battle cries could be heard as they rushed towards the immobile war machines. Hundreds of men and women charged across the no man's land, ropes and grappling hooks in hand.

'They're going for them,' Maksym murmured into his comms, his eyes fixed on the unfolding scene.

The first war machine, standing frozen at the edge of the battlefield, was swarmed by defenders. Ropes were thrown over its frame, latching onto joints and armour plates. Dozens of soldiers pulled with all their might, straining to topple the lifeless giant. For a moment, it seemed impossible, but then, with a deafening crash, the first T90 toppled to the ground, dust and dirt billowing in its wake.

Cheers erupted from the defenders as they rushed to the next machine, and the process repeated. One by one, the mighty war machines that had once dominated the battlefield were pulled down.

Dimitri watched in awe as the defenders worked with feverish determination, climbing the fallen machines, prying open access panels, and reprogramming their systems. The Signals drone had given them more than just a temporary reprieve – it had handed them the key to turning the tide of the war.

'They're reprogramming them,' Dimitri said, his voice filled with wonder. 'They're taking control.'

'That was always the plan,' Maksym replied, eyes glinting with a new sense of hope. 'We didn't just stop the Rusviet's attack. We've just given Ukraine an army of their own.'

Across the battlefield, more and more machines were claimed by the defenders. As the war machines began to rise again, this time under the control of Ukrainian forces, the balance of power shifted dramatically. What was once a hopeless defence had become a full-scale counteroffensive.

'This is just the beginning,' Maksym said, his voice steady. 'With these machines on our side, we have a real chance to win this war.'

Dimitri looked out across the vast horizon, the lights of Lviv flickering in the distance. The city had survived, but more than that, it now had hope.

'We changed everything tonight,' he said quietly.

Maksym looked at him, a spark of pride in his eyes. 'And the world will never be the same again.'

As they turned towards Lviv, the drone's final signal still spreading across the Rusviet's forces, Dimitri – instead of feeling a sense of calm – felt a foreboding sense that something wasn't quite right.

At that moment, a large craft, sleek and dark, appeared above them, emerging from the haze of war. Its massive engines pulsed with a deep vibration as it hovered above the terrain. Dimitri's breath caught in his throat as he looked up and spotted the insignia emblazoned on its side: a gleaming red star, encircled by the black crest of the High Commissariat.

A piercing whistle split the air. Dimitri's heart lurched: missiles streaked down from the craft above. There was a split second of eerie silence, then the world exploded in a deafening roar. The force of the blast was like nothing he had ever felt – pure, violent power that rocked the earth beneath him.

Sova shuddered as the missiles struck. Dimitri's hands flew to the controls, but it was too late. Sova's massive frame tilted, her systems flickering under the impact, and with a bone-rattling crash, she was slammed into the ground. The cockpit shook violently, and Dimitri was thrown hard against the harness, the breath knocked from his lungs.

The noise was overwhelming – metal grinding, stone crumbling, the roar of fire and smoke all around him. He could barely hear his own thoughts over the cacophony. Sova, a titan of steel and power, lay helpless, sprawled across the rubble-strewn ground. Dimitri could feel the vibrations of the collapse through his entire body, a raw, gut-wrenching sensation.

Through the smoke and noise, Dimitri's vision blurred, his ears ringing. He saw Katya struggling to regain her footing, only to be sent sprawling by the second wave of the blast. The Sentinels, too, were hurled like ragdolls by the force of the explosion, smashing into the dirt.

Everything around him fell into a disorienting silence, as if the world had momentarily stopped. Smoke billowed across the battlefield, and the acrid scent of burning metal filled the air.

Dimitri scrambled to regain his bearings, his heart racing. The Sentinels, despite the blast, were already recovering, shaking off debris as their weapons came to life. They began firing back at the craft, their Longbow rifles and miniguns both rattling as they aimed for its vulnerable spots.

But the craft wasn't retreating.

Sova lay motionless from the missile attack, systems flickering, as the craft lowered itself closer to the ground. Dimitri's eyes widened as grappling hooks shot out from its underside, latching onto Sova's frame with a series of sharp *clangs*. The cables tightened, and slowly, Sova began to lift off the ground, her enormous form dangling beneath the craft like a captured beast.

From inside Katya's cockpit, Maksym had a clear view of what was unfolding.

Maksym gritted his teeth, his hands moving swiftly over Katya's controls as she struggled to her feet. The blast had knocked her off balance, but with a groaning effort, she rose, wobbling slightly as she found her footing. Maksym wasn't about to let Sova and Dimitri be taken without a fight. He pushed Katya forward, her lumbering steps echoing through the ground as she closed the distance to Sova.

'Come on,' Maksym muttered, driving Katya with everything she had left. With a final surge of power, Katya lunged forward, her long arms reaching out and grabbing onto Sova's legs. The impact slowed Sova's ascent, and for a moment, both machines suspended by the powerful cables pulling Sova upward.

Maksym popped open Katya's cockpit hatch, the wind and debris whipping around him as he yelled up at Sova. 'Dimitri! Get out! Now!'

From his vantage point, Maksym could see Dimitri inside Sova's cockpit, dazed and disoriented. His movements were sluggish as he struggled to process what was happening. 'Dimitri!' Maksym shouted again, his voice cutting through the chaos. 'Get out, or they'll take you too!'

Slowly, Dimitri's hand moved, and with a click, Sova's cockpit hatch began to open. Maksym didn't wait. With Katya still gripping Sova's leg, Maksym scrambled out of

Katya's cockpit and climbed up Sova's frame, the cables straining as the two giants hung precariously in midair.

Maksym reached the open cockpit, oblivious to the chaotic gunfire as the Sentinels below attempted to destroy the craft carrying them all. He hoisted Dimitri over his shoulder, the boy still dazed, and began the precarious descent down Sova's frame. The metallic surface was slick with dust and debris from the explosion, but Maksym's grip was firm as he scaled down, his muscles straining under the weight.

Below them, the Sentinels continued to unleash a relentless barrage of firepower at the ascending craft, their guns blazing as they tried to bring it down. The heavy thrum of their weapons filled the air, lighting up the battlefield beneath the darkened sky. Each burst of gunfire struck the underbelly, but the craft remained undeterred, holding onto Sova and Katya.

Maksym's heart raced as he moved. He kept one arm wrapped tightly around Dimitri, who clung to him with weak hands, still recovering from the missile attack that knocked over Sova.

When they reached the base of Sova's frame, Maksym jumped the final few feet, landing heavily inside Katya's open cockpit, with Dimitri falling onto the seat beside him. Without wasting a moment, Maksym slammed the cockpit shut, sealing them inside.

Maksym's eyes widened as he realized what was coming, but there was no time to react. A missile streaked down from the High Commissariat's craft and slammed directly into Katya's chest with an earth-shattering impact.

The explosion rocked the cockpit, sending Maksym and Dimitri crashing against its walls. Katya's grip on Sova was broken by the force of the impact. 'Hold on!' Maksym yelled as Katya hit the ground, her systems sparking and groaning from the damage.

Through the viewport, Dimitri watched in horror as the craft began its ascent, pulling Sova higher into the air. The grappling hooks held fast as the craft moved steadily eastward, above the forest.

'We have to stop them,' Dimitri gasped, trying to sit up, but the force of the fall had left him shaken.

Maksym's fists clenched as he watched helplessly. The red insignia of the High Commissariat gleamed coldly as the craft rose above the treetops in the distance, Sova suspended beneath it like a trophy. The cables tightened, and with a final roar from its engines, the craft moved off into the distance, disappearing over the dense forest and out of view.

'They've taken her,' Maksym muttered through gritted teeth, his chest tight with frustration. Katya's systems struggled to reboot, but the damage from the missile had left her immobilized for now.

All they could do was watch as Sova was carried away, lost in the sky.

The cockpit was quiet, save for the soft hum of Katya's damaged systems trying to restore themselves. Maksym leaned back against the seat, wiping sweat from his brow. Dimitri sat beside him, face pale and eyes wide, still processing the whirlwind of events. The silence between them lingered, heavy with the weight of what they had just lost.

'Sova ...' Dimitri's voice broke through the quiet, laced with grief and anger. 'We have to get her back.'

Maksym nodded, his expression hard. 'We will,' he said firmly. 'We'll find her, no matter how far they take her. And we won't stop there.'

Dimitri looked up, confused. 'What do you mean?'

Maksym's gaze shifted to the viewport, where the treetops of the forest stretched endlessly below them. His jaw clenched. 'We're not just getting Sova back. The Rusviet Empire has taken too much from too many people. They've taken your parents, Dimitri. They've taken entire cities. It's time we take something back.'

Dimitri's heart pounded at the mention of his parents. He had always hoped they were alive, somewhere out there. Maksym's words reignited that hope. He straightened in his seat. 'Then we'll find them. Sova … my parents. And we'll make the Rusviet Empire pay for everything they've done.'

They sat in silence again, the vastness of what lay ahead settling over them. It wasn't going to be easy, but there was no turning back now.

'This isn't over,' Maksym said quietly, almost to himself. 'Not by a long shot.'

Dimitri nodded, the fire of a new mission burning in his chest. 'We'll find them,' he whispered. 'And we'll make sure the Rusviet Empire falls – once and for all.'

Appendix - Forged for War: The Machines of SOVA

Sova - Advanced War Machine – series a (AWMa)

Sova (Ukrainian for 'Owl') is a cutting-edge, co-piloted AI war machine built for the Ukrainian resistance. True to her name, she is optimized for nocturnal operations, excelling in both front-line combat and reconnaissance. Powered by a nuclear core, Sova combines raw firepower with agility, executing rapid manoeuvres that defy her imposing size. Her rarity—one of the last of her kind— has elevated her to near-legendary status on the battlefield, a symbol of resilience in a war dominated by machines.

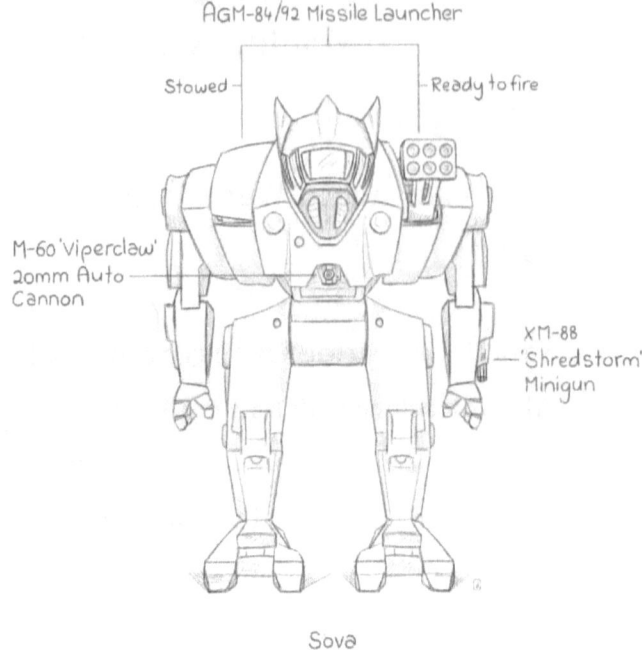

AGM-84/92 Missile Launcher

Stowed —

— Ready to fire

M-60 'Viperclaw' 20mm Auto Cannon

XM-88 — 'Shredstorm' Minigun

Sova

Primary Weapon Systems:

M-60 'Viperclaw' 20mm Auto Cannon (Chest Mounted)

The 'Viperclaw' is a 20mm auto cannon mounted in Sova's chest, capable of delivering continuous high-velocity fire for up to 20 seconds. Its high-explosive rounds are designed to tear through both infantry and armoured targets with ease. The Viperclaw can fire 600 rounds per minute, unleashing a devastating storm of firepower before requiring a short cooldown period.

Fire Rate: 600 rounds per minute.

Ammunition: Armour-piercing high-explosive rounds.

Capacity: 200 rounds per burst, with reloads stored in internal chambers.

Effective Range: 2.5 kilometres (2,500 meters).

Usage: Ideal for shredding through enemy lines or taking down heavily armoured opponents.

XM-88 'Shredstorm' Minigun (Left Arm Embedded)

The 'Shredstorm' minigun, embedded in Sova's left arm, is a high-speed rotary weapon capable of firing at an astounding 2,000 rounds per minute. This minigun is designed for close-quarters combat and infantry suppression, making it the perfect tool for clearing enemy forces and supporting rapid assaults. The 'Shredstorm' can switch between incendiary, armour-piercing, and standard rounds, depending on the target.

Fire Rate: 2,000 rounds per minute.

Ammunition: 7.62mm rounds (standard, incendiary, or armour-piercing).

Capacity: 1,000 rounds per engagement, with internal magazines.

Effective Range: 1.2 kilometres (1,200 meters).

Usage: Best for engaging enemy infantry, light vehicles, and suppressing close-range threats.

AGM-84/92 Missile Launcher (Shoulder Mounted)

The AGM-84/92 missile launcher is capable of firing both surface-to-surface and surface-to-air missiles. Each launcher (mounted on both shoulders) holds up to six missiles, and Sova can reload her supply from a nearby cache if necessary. The system can lock onto multiple targets, allowing for precise, long-range strikes on enemy tanks, fortifications, or aircraft.

Missile Types:

Surface-to-Surface: AGM-84 'Thunderclaw' anti-armour missiles.

Surface-to-Air: AGM-92 'Dragonspear' heat-seeking missiles.

Capacity: 12 missiles (6 per shoulder).

Effective Range: Surface-to-Surface: 8 kilometres. Surface-to-Air: 15 kilometres.

Usage: Long-range strikes against heavily armoured targets, enemy fortifications, or aerial threats.

Secondary Systems:

AEW (Advanced Electronic Warfare) Suite: Equipped with systems that can jam enemy communications, radar, and targeting systems, providing an edge in tactical engagements.

Adaptive Plating: Sova's armour can dynamically adjust to the threat level, hardening against kinetic and energy-based weapons when under attack.

A12 Sentinel (Ukrainian Resistance)

The A12 Sentinel is a highly advanced, humanoid war robot designed by the Ukrainian Resistance to serve in both offensive and defensive operations. These Sentinels combine cutting-edge weaponry with adaptive AI to provide critical battlefield support. Despite their mechanical nature, A12 Sentinels possess an eerily human appearance, allowing for more seamless communication and camaraderie.

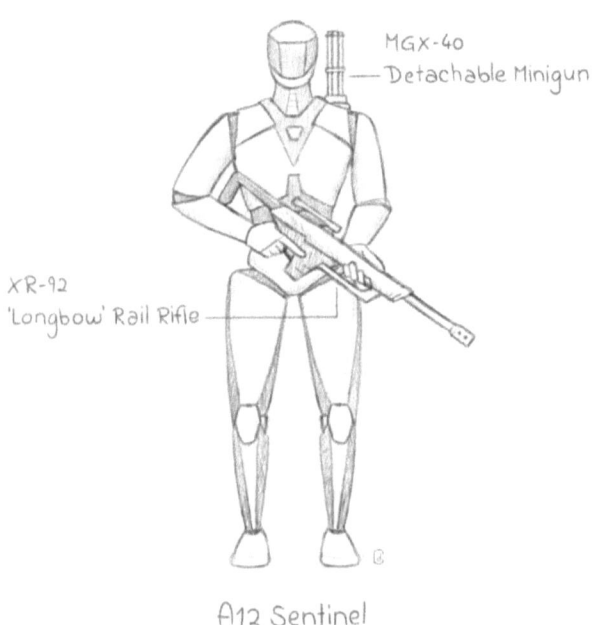

A12 Sentinel

268

Primary Weapon Systems:

'Longbow' XR-92 Rail Rifle (Primary Weapon)

The Longbow XR-92 is a powerful rail rifle that fires high-velocity, explosive shells capable of penetrating enemy armour and causing widespread damage. Designed for long-range precision, this weapon allows the A12 Sentinel to engage targets from a distance, often taking out enemy vehicles, fortified positions, or heavily armoured units with a single well-placed shot.

Fire Rate: Semi-automatic, with a brief charge time between shots.

Ammunition: Explosive kinetic shells, designed to detonate on impact.

Effective Range: 3 kilometres (3,000 meters).

Key Usage: The Longbow excels at long-range engagements, providing sniper-like capabilities that can change the course of a battle by eliminating high-value targets from afar.

MGX-40 Detachable Minigun (Secondary Weapon)

The MGX-40 is a detachable minigun, capable of autonomous fire or perching on the Sentinel's shoulder for continuous suppression. Its high rate of fire makes it ideal for cutting down enemy infantry or providing cover fire in chaotic battlefield situations. When deployed autonomously, the Minigun can act as a mobile turret, defending a strategic point or laying down suppressive fire while the Sentinel advances.

Fire Rate: 4,000 rounds per minute.

Ammunition: Standard armour-piercing rounds, with optional incendiary or high-explosive shells.

Effective Range: 1 kilometre (1,000 meters).

Secondary Systems:

Adaptive Combat AI: The A12 Sentinel's AI allows it to learn and adapt to battlefield conditions, making tactical decisions based on real-time data. It can adjust its combat approach depending on the nature of the enemy or environmental conditions.

Autonomous Support Mode: When necessary, Sentinels can be deployed autonomously to act as defensive units, providing suppression fire, covering retreats, or holding strategic positions.

Nano-Weave Armour: The A12's outer shell is made from a nano-weave composite that offers superior protection against both ballistic and energy-based attacks, while remaining lightweight enough to allow for rapid movement.

Stealth Capability: Equipped with limited stealth technology, the A12 Sentinel can briefly cloak itself to reposition on the battlefield, making it harder for enemy forces to track and engage.

T90 VX 'Volk' (Rusviet)

The T90 VX 'Volk' (translated as 'Wolf') is the Rusviet Empire's primary battle robot, designed to crush enemy defences with overwhelming brute force. The Volk is heavily armoured and equipped with an array of destructive weapons, making it a formidable adversary.

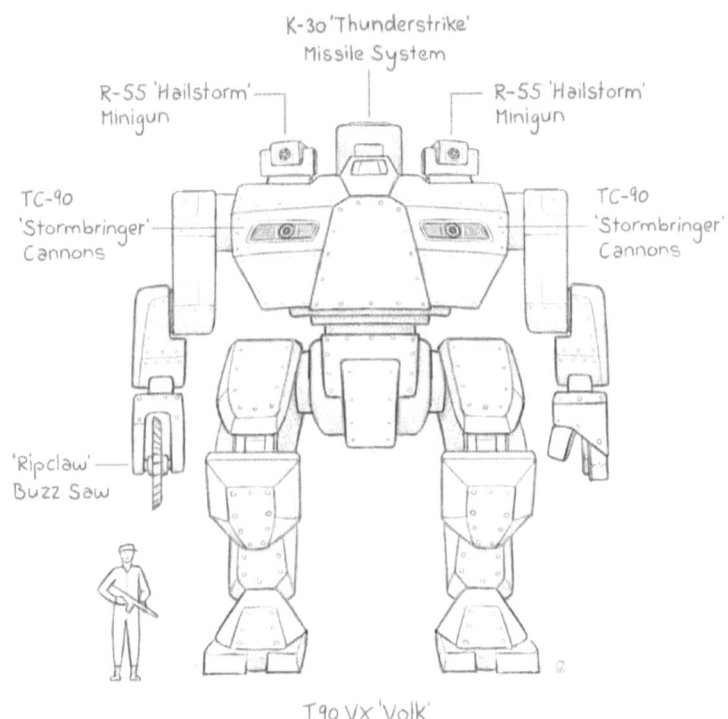

K-30 'Thunderstrike' Missile System

R-55 'Hailstorm' Minigun

R-55 'Hailstorm' Minigun

TC-90 'Stormbringer' Cannons

TC-90 'Stormbringer' Cannons

'Ripclaw' Buzz Saw

T90 VX 'Volk'

Primary Weapon Systems:

TC-90 Twin 'Stormbringer' Cannons (Chest-Mounted)

The Stormbringer twin cannons are mounted in the Volk's chest, capable of unleashing heavy firepower at medium and long ranges. These cannons fire high-explosive shells that can obliterate both infantry and armoured vehicles. With their chest-mounted position, the cannons provide a wide firing arc, allowing the Volk to engage multiple enemies simultaneously.

Fire Rate: 120 rounds per minute (combined for both cannons).

Ammunition: High-explosive, armour-piercing rounds.

Effective Range: 3 kilometres (3,000 meters).

Key Usage: Primarily used for bombarding enemy fortifications and armoured units, the Stormbringer cannons give the Volk unmatched destructive power on the battlefield.

'Ripclaw' Buzz Saw (Right Fist)

The Ripclaw buzz saw is mounted in the Volk's right fist, designed for close-quarter combat and breaching fortified structures. Capable of spinning at incredibly high speeds, the Ripclaw can slice through metal, concrete, and flesh with ease, making it ideal for finishing off crippled vehicles or dispatching enemy soldiers at close range.

Key Usage: Used as a last-resort weapon when the Volk closes in on enemy positions or for tearing through defensive fortifications. The buzz saw is particularly terrifying in urban warfare, where tight quarters allow the Volk to engage enemies up close.

R-55 Twin 'Hailstorm' Miniguns (Shoulder-Mounted)

The Hailstorm miniguns are mounted on the Volk's shoulders, providing suppression fire and close-range anti-infantry capabilities.

Fire Rate: 6,000 rounds per minute (combined for both miniguns).

Ammunition: 12.7mm armour-piercing rounds, with the option for incendiary and tracer rounds.

Effective Range: 1.5 kilometres (1,500 meters).

Key Usage: The Hailstorm miniguns are used for crowd control, infantry suppression, and creating a deadly field of fire around the Volk to protect it from infantry assaults.

K-30 'Thunderstrike' Missile System (Back-Mounted)

The Thunderstrike missile launcher is mounted on the Volk's back, capable of firing both surface-to-surface and surface-to-air missiles. The system can carry a mix of missiles for anti-armour and anti-aircraft purposes, making the Volk a versatile threat to both ground and air targets.

Missile Types:

Surface-to-Surface: Long-range anti-armour missiles capable of penetrating tank armour and fortified positions.

Surface-to-Air: Heat-seeking missiles for engaging enemy drones and aircraft.

Capacity: 8 missiles total (4 surface-to-surface, 4 surface-to-air).

Effective Range: Surface-to-Surface: 6 kilometres (6,000 meters). Surface-to-Air: 12 kilometres (12,000 meters).

Secondary Systems:

Self-Repair Protocols: The Volk is equipped with basic self-repair systems that allow it to patch minor damage during battle, increasing its endurance on the front lines.

Combat AI: The Volk's AI is programmed for brute force tactics, prioritising direct engagements and overwhelming enemy defences. The AI can manage its various weapon systems independently, allowing the Volk to engage multiple targets simultaneously.

S10 'Velociraptor' (Rusviet)

The S10 'Velociraptor' is one of the most agile and fast-moving units in the Rusviet Empire's mechanised forces. Standing at the height of an adult human, the Velociraptor's slim, angular frame is eerily reminiscent of the predatory dinosaur it takes its name from. Engineered for speed and precision, the Velociraptor excels in skirmishes and patrols, often deployed to quickly engage enemy infantry and light armour.

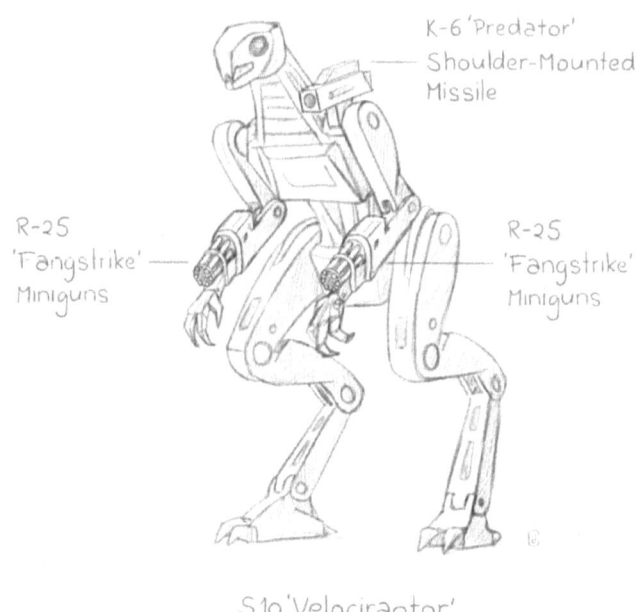

K-6 'Predator' Shoulder-Mounted Missile

R-25 'Fangstrike' Miniguns

R-25 'Fangstrike' Miniguns

S10 'Velociraptor'

Primary Weapon Systems:

R-25 Twin 'Fangstrike' Miniguns (Arm-Mounted)

The Fangstrike miniguns are mounted directly into the arms of the Velociraptor, delivering rapid-fire barrages against infantry and light vehicles. Capable of independent targeting, the miniguns can engage multiple foes at once, providing devastating suppressive fire.

Fire Rate: 3,000 rounds per minute (per minigun).

Ammunition: 5.56mm armour-piercing rounds, effective against infantry and light vehicles.

Effective Range: 1 kilometre (1,000 meters).

Key Usage: Primarily used for cutting down infantry and providing suppression during quick strikes, the Fangstrike miniguns are the Velociraptor's primary tools for combat.

K-6 'Predator' Shoulder-Mounted Missile (Variant Loadout)

The Predator K-6 missile system is a variant loadout carried by select Velociraptors for heavier engagements. Equipped with a single shoulder-mounted surface-to-surface missile, the Predator is designed to handle armoured targets or fortified positions. However, not all Velociraptors are equipped with this missile, as they are typically reserved for specific missions requiring additional firepower.

Missile Type: Surface-to-surface high-explosive missile.

Capacity: 1 reloadable missile.

Effective Range: 2 kilometres (2,000 meters).

Secondary Systems:

Tactical AI: The Velociraptor's AI is built for quick decision-making in high-stress environments, relying on reactive combat instincts rather than strategic planning. This allows it to thrive in fast-paced skirmishes, though it lacks the advanced coordination of more complex AI units.

Enhanced Mobility: With powerful servos and an agile frame, the Velociraptor can execute rapid manoeuvres, including sudden directional changes, sprints, and strafes, making it hard to hit in combat.

Thermal and Night Vision: The unit is equipped with advanced thermal and night vision capabilities, allowing it to operate effectively in low-visibility environments, including smoke-filled battlefields or nighttime operations.

Sui 77 'Red Viper' (Rusviet)

The Sui 77 'Red Viper' is a specialised air attack drone developed by the Rusviet Empire, designed for aerial bombardment and ground suppression. Highly manoeuvrable and difficult to target, the Red Viper excels in hit-and-run tactics, striking enemy fortifications and retreating before counterattacks can be mounted. Known for its precision and speed, the Sui 77 plays a vital role in Rusviet air superiority, harassing both ground forces and air units with devastating firepower.

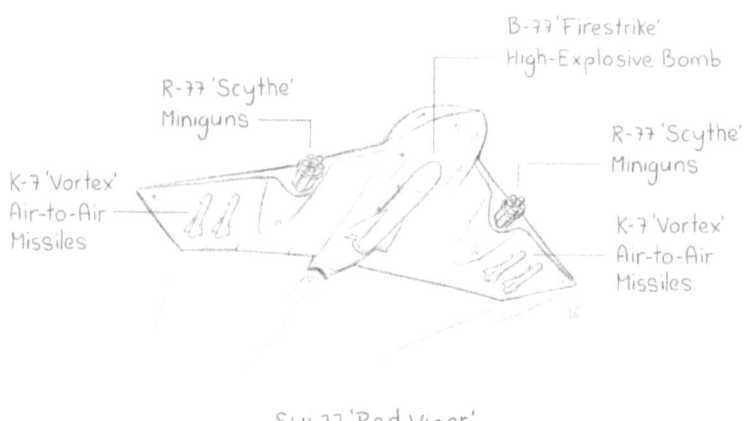

Sui 77 'Red Viper'

Primary Weapon Systems:

B-77 'Firestrike' High-Explosive Bomb (Payload)

The Firestrike is a single, large high-explosive bomb carried beneath the Sui 77. Designed for maximum destruction, this bomb is deployed during precision bombardments of enemy fortifications, armoured columns, or critical infrastructure. The Firestrike is capable of levelling buildings or incapacitating groups of armoured vehicles in a single drop.

Effective Range: High-altitude deployment allows for precision drops on targets up to 10 kilometres away.

R-77 Twin 'Scythe' Miniguns (Forward-Mounted)

The Scythe miniguns are mounted on the front of the Red Viper, designed to unleash a torrent of rounds onto ground forces or aerial targets. Capable of firing at an exceptionally high rate, these miniguns are perfect for strafing runs, quickly cutting down infantry or suppressing anti-aircraft emplacements.

Fire Rate: 5,000 rounds per minute (combined).

Ammunition: 7.62mm armour-piercing rounds.

Effective Range: 1.5 kilometres (1,500 meters).

K-7 'Vortex' Air-to-Air Missiles (Optional Loadout)

The Vortex missiles provide the Sui 77 with anti-air capabilities, allowing it to engage enemy aircraft or drones during aerial combat. While not all Red Vipers are equipped with these missiles, those that are can lock onto and destroy enemy air units from long distances, giving the Rusviet Empire a formidable air defence option.

Missile Type: Heat-seeking air-to-air missiles.

Capacity: 2 missiles (1 per wing).

Effective Range: 8 kilometres (8,000 meters).

Key Usage: The Vortex AA-7 missiles are primarily deployed on Red Vipers in high-threat zones, where enemy air resistance is anticipated. These missiles allow the drone to take on enemy fighters and drones, maintaining air superiority during key operations.

Secondary Systems:

Evasive Manoeuvring AI: The Sui 77 is equipped with advanced flight AI that allows it to perform sharp turns, rolls, and rapid ascents or descents to avoid incoming fire. This makes the Red Viper notoriously difficult to target with ground-based anti-aircraft systems.

Stealth Coating: The drone's body is covered in a special radar-dampening material, making it harder to detect and track on enemy radar systems. While not fully invisible, the stealth coating allows it to close the distance on targets before they can fully engage.

Recon Capabilities: In addition to its combat role, the Red Viper is equipped with cameras and sensors that allow it to perform reconnaissance, providing valuable intel on enemy positions before launching an attack.

Afterword from Stephen Beath

As a self published debut author, the journey to writing this book has been 10 years in the making. I had been tossing around an idea where an advanced AI robot lay buried in a hill, forgotten, while a war raged on. I guess life got in the way and the concept remained buried, like the robot itself.

Fast forward to last year. As the conflict in Ukraine dominated the news, the story of the buried Robot on a distant planet moved to a more grounded, near future story set in Ukraine. I felt that it would be too political referring to Russia as the invaders, I shifted the storyline to the Rusviet Empire, which succeeds the current political arrangement with Putin at the helm. To add some plausible continuity, I decided that it was countless peace treaties that were broken between present day and 2036 where the story is set.

At its heart, Sova is about more than just battles and AI machines. It's about finding strength in adversity, the bond between unlikely allies, and hope in the face of overwhelming odds.

The journey of bringing this story to life has been deeply personal for me. It combines my love of sci-fi, my interest in geopolitics, and the inspiration I draw from my son William's experience with Beckwith Weidermann, and his determination and courage.

I'd like to express my thanks to Charlene J Moore who has been so helpful (and patient) with editing this book. And to Chris Davidson, a supremely talented Illustrator and dear friend of mine. And last, but by no means least, to Sabrina Beath, beautiful wife and constant supporter who always backs me with my projects, and is the first one to say JFDI (Just F'ing Do It) whenever I have doubts. I do hope you enjoy this book.

Want to stay connected, you'll find me on Bluesky @stevieb73.bsky.social
Wholesale/distribution enquires to:
stephen.beath73@gmail.com

www.ingramcontent.com/pod-product-compliance
Lightning Source LLC
Chambersburg PA
CBHW022146170626
46807CB00005B/2101